STARING INTO THE
EYES OF DEATH

In pursuit of the evil magician Zed, you, your new friend, Saffron, and your faithful pseudo-dragon, Hinoki, have stumbled upon a fierce many-headed hydra in the dismal mists of the Great Swamp. Its tiny cold eyes stare straight into yours, and it appears ready to strike at any moment!

What will you do?

1) "Maybe I can fight it." If this is what you decide, turn to page 140.

2) "Maybe it hasn't seen us yet and we can run away." If this is your decision, turn to page 77.

3) "Maybe I can use my magical Ring of Wishes." If you want to use the ring, turn to page 97.

4) "Maybe I can trick it." If you think you can trick the hydra, turn to page 48.

Whichever path you pick, you are sure to find adventure as you battle the mighty
DRAGON OF DOOM

DRAGON OF DOOM

BY ROSE ESTES

A DUNGEONS & DRAGONS™ Adventure Book

Cover Art by Clyde Caldwell
Interior Art by Harry Quinn

TSR, Inc.
PRODUCTS OF YOUR IMAGINATION™

This book is for Sabrina,
Kimberley, Brad, and Craig

Distributed to the book trade in the United States by Random House, Inc.,
and in Canada by Random House of Canada, Ltd.
Distributed in the United Kingdom by TSR (UK), Ltd.
Distributed to the toy and hobby trade by regional distributors.

DUNGEONS & DRAGONS, ENDLESS QUEST, and PICK A PATH TO
ADVENTURE are trademarks owned by TSR, Inc.

D&D is a registered trademark owned by TSR, Inc.

First printing: November, 1983
Printed in the United States of America
Library of Congress Catalog Card Number: 83-51039
ISBN: 0-88038-100-0

9 8 7 6 5 4 3 2 1

TSR, Inc.
P.O. Box 756
Lake Geneva, WI 53147

TSR (UK), Ltd.
The Mill, Rathmore Road
Cambridge, CB1 4AD
United Kingdom

You are about to set off on an adventure in which YOU will meet many dangers—and face many decisions. YOUR choices will determine how the story turns out. So be careful . . . you must choose wisely!

Do not read this book from beginning to end! Instead, as you are faced with a decision, follow the instructions and keep turning to the pages where your choices lead you until you come to an end. At any point, YOUR choice could bring success—or disaster!

You can read DRAGON OF DOOM many times, with many different results, so if you make an unwise choice, go back to the beginning and start again!

Good luck on YOUR adventure!

In this story, you are Morgan, a young magic-user who has just received an urgent summons to appear before the venerable Council of Nine. Although you do not know the reason for the mysterious summons, you hope with all your heart that you are about to be entrusted with your first important quest.

But first share the thoughts of someone—no, some THING—something very big, very sinister, and very terrifying. . . .

The great dragon stirs restlessly in its sleep, trying to ignore the summons that whispers in its ear. Gold, silver, and jewels caress its body as it burrows deeper into the pile of treasure. But the message continues to echo in its head, "Come to me, I command you, O Shen, great Dragon of Doom. I have uttered the secret words, and you must do my bidding. Come, and you will have riches beyond belief. I seek revenge upon the world, and you are my weapon. Come to me now."

One huge golden eye opens slowly. Black scales ripple up and down the dragon's immense length as the great creature stirs. The message repeats over and over inside its head, summoning, commanding, demanding.

Shaking its massive black head back and forth, Shen crawls forth from the warm, dark cave where it has slumbered for the last four centuries. Blinking wearily, it peers down upon the world it had left behind and finds it unchanged.

Slowly the dragon unfurls its enormous wings and stretches the muscles in its massive body. Opening its gaping mouth, Shen looses a roar that singes the earth below.

"It is wrong that I must serve man and his paltry needs," Shen rumbles. "Man should serve me—Shen, the Dragon of Doom. There is only one like me in the entire universe. Where I am, there is death. I am supreme. I am Shen!"

Stiff with age and sleep, the dragon spreads its enormous wings and launches itself into the air toward the summoning message. The sky grows black with the mighty dragon's passage, and wherever its shadow touches, there life ceases to exist. And word spreads that Shen, the Dragon of Doom, is once more loose in the land.

Please turn the page.

You stand before the Council of Nine, barely able to control your excitement, though it is mingled with fear.

"Morgan," quavers the voice of Fazad, the eldest of the council, "we have summoned you here today to propose to you a mission of great importance.

"Nine hundred and ninety-nine years ago, your venerable ancestor, Zed the Zealous, Supreme Magic-user and member of the Council of Nine, was banished to Bald Mountain as punishment for practicing forbidden magic. His period of repentence will soon end.

"You are his closest living relative and our youngest magic-user. Therefore, we wish you to travel to Bald Mountain to escort him home in honor. What say you?"

Your mouth grows dry and your heart pounds in your chest. Your mother's dying words echo in your mind: "Morgan, you must do whatever you can to help your uncle. And remember how fortunate you are to have a pseudo-dragon. Treat it well. It shares your thoughts and will share its wisdom with you. Never think of it as merely a small dragon who can mind-link. One day it may help you to remove the black mark against our family's name. . . ."

"Honorable sirs, I am honored to do so," you say. As you step forward, your staff becomes tangled between your legs, and it is only with difficulty that you catch your balance.

"Are you all right, young Morgan?" asks a council member.

"Y-Yes, sir," you answer, growing red. "It's just that sometimes I'm a little clumsy."

"Sometimes you even fall on ME," hisses a small voice in your ear as eight sharp little claws grip your shoulder.

"May Hinoki go with me?"

"The little pseudo-dragon?" queries Baron Beta. "I see no reason why not, as long as it does not hinder your quest. The day of Zed's release draws near. It is most important that you be there the moment the time barrier is lifted. It would not do to have Zed think we have forgotten him. Present him with our salutations and tell him that we await his return with great happiness. A fitting celebration awaits his return. You must also give him his ring of wishes, which was held in safekeeping for him."

Holding the magic ring carefully, you bow to the council and make your way out of the chamber, trying hard not to stumble.

"As long as I don't hinder your quest," chuckles Hinoki. "Who do they think keeps you on your feet most of the time?"

"Come on, Hinoki. I'm not that bad," you say, eyeing the small creature, which looks just like a miniature red dragon.

"You're not that good, either. Remember that time when I was still in the egg and you fell on me and nearly squashed me?"

"Oh, Hinoki! I've apologized for that a million times. It was an accident!"

"That's okay. I like you anyhow. You're not so bad for a human," Hinoki murmurs as he nibbles on your ear with his sharp little teeth. "When do we leave?"

"First thing in the morning. I don't really know where Bald Mountain is. All I know is that it's somewhere to the north."

"You are going to get a map, aren't you?"

"Of course I am. You don't think I'd just wander off in the general direction, do you? . . . Never mind. Don't answer that!"

"You don't prepare fully enough," says Hinoki. "You should lay your plans ahead of time, so that there will be as few unpleasant surprises as possible."

"But that's boring," you say. "I am a magic-user, you know. And I have very good intuition. I can always tell the best thing to do in a bad situation. Anyone can follow a boring map. I prefer my own methods."

"You may be a magic-user, but let me remind you that you've only just graduated. You don't know everything yet."

"I know all the important stuff! I even got honors on my written exams. And I have my Uncle Zed's ring."

"You wouldn't use it, would you?" Hinoki asks, horrified.

"Not unless I had to," you answer.

"It's too powerful for you. And your uncle would be very angry!"

"He'd understand," you reply smoothly. But inwardly, you are uncertain.

Early next morning, while the dew is still on the grass, you and Hinoki pass out of the castle and head north toward Bald Mountain.

The trip passes without incident until the morning of the third day.

"We should have spotted the mountain by now," insists Hinoki. "I'm going to fly to the top of that knoll and take a look around. You stay here."

"You're as bad as a mother," you groan. "I'm supposed to be in charge. I'll go, too!" And ignoring Hinoki's protests, you climb to the top of the rocky knoll.

"That must be it," you say, pointing toward a black peak that thrusts up into the cold mountain mists. "It sure looks unfriendly. I'll bet Uncle Zed will be glad to see me."

"Be careful on the way down," says Hinoki.

"Oh, stop fussing! I'll be just fi—" You feel a loose rock shift under your foot, and you begin to slide. Desperately you try to regain your balance. Too late, you see the large black rock rising up before you, and then there is a sickening thud and the world goes black.

"Morgan! Morgan! Wake up!" cries a tiny voice inside your head, and you see a tiny pinpoint of light. Vaguely you watch the dot, and slowly it grows larger and the voice grows louder.

"Morgan! Wake up! We'll be late for the time barrier!" insists the voice.

Lazily you listen to the words and wonder at their meaning. Moving seems much too difficult. Maybe you'll go back to sleep.

"If you don't wake up, I shall leave you and

go on by myself. And don't blame me if the dire wolves eat you."

Eaten by dire wolves? Hmmm. That doesn't sound like much fun. Slowly you open one eye to see Hinoki peering into your face.

"I thought you'd finally gotten yourself killed this time," says the pseudo-dragon. "Come on. Either you get up, or I'm leaving. We've lost too much time, thanks to your clever way of descending a cliff."

"I—I must have knocked myself out," you say, rubbing a painful lump on the top of your head. "How long was I out?"

"All day and all night," says Hinoki, rubbing his muzzle your cheek. "I was scared to death you would die."

"That long? Come on! We've got to get going! Maybe if I walk all night I can get there before the time barrier lifts!"

But even though you walk as fast as you can, you know that you are too late before you even reach the mountain.

"Look, Hinoki! Smoke!" you say, pointing to the plume of black smoke that stains the northern sky.

All that day, the signs grow worse. Dead birds, with greasy black smoke coating their plumage, litter the ground. Then you begin to see other small creatures—mice, snakes, rabbits, all with scorch marks on their bodies.

"I don't like the looks of this," you mutter. "Hinoki, are you receiving any mind thoughts?"

"Fright. Pain. Death. Blackness," says your

pseudo-dragon nervously.

"If we link our minds, we'll be twice as powerful. Let's try it and see what we can see. Maybe Uncle Zed is hurt."

Sitting down on a large rock, you perch Hinoki on your knees and touch his head to your own. Slowly you calm your heartbeat and breathe in and out with the pseudo-dragon as you look into the gold depths of his eyes. Gradually, a calming warmth steals over you, and you enter a trancelike state. Your black pupils open wider and wider until you see a small, huddled figure lying on the ground. As you watch, the figure stirs and pain washes over you. You flinch from the pain, and the picture fades.

"Did you see him? It's Uncle Zed, and he's hurt! We've got to get there as soon as possible! Something terrible has happened!" you say in a rush.

For the remainder of that day and the following night, you walk, with fear your constant companion.

"If something has happened to Uncle Zed, the council will never forgive me," you say. Hinoki is strangely silent.

On the morning of the fifth day, you stand high on a mountain pass and look upon destruction that can scarcely be imagined. Bald Mountain rises straight up before you, blasted barren and black, as though struck by all the lightning in the world. Charred remains of forests cast smoke into the mists. Rocks and boulders lie smashed, as though shattered by a giant

hammer. In places, the very ground is ripped asunder, with molten rock bubbling and fuming from the wide cracks.

"Maybe he's still alive," you whisper as you hurry toward the desolate scene. Following a narrow path, you wind your way up toward an opening in the mountain. Pushing your way past the fallen rubble, you enter a deep cave and rush to the side of a small crumpled figure lying broken on the cold stone floor.

"Uncle Zed!" you cry as you gently turn the figure's face toward you.

"No," whispers the man. "Not Zed. Cycas. I was Zed's servant."

"What happened? Is Zed all right? Is he still alive?" you ask urgently.

"Alive? Yes, he's alive," gasps the man as he gives a choking laugh.

"What's funny? Where is my uncle? I've come to bring him home. There's going to be a celebration and speeches, and he'll be returned to his place of honor. What's happened to him? Tell me!"

A terrible grimace crosses the man's face, and his body shakes with silent laughter.

"So they've forgiven him, have they? Well, I'm afraid it's too late for that. Did they really think he would take his banishment lightly? Not Zed. He used all his magic skills to call upon the powers of darkness to aid him in his revenge."

"Revenge! What revenge? He's forgiven!"

"You may have forgiven him, but he has not

forgiven those who banished him. They will pay dearly for what they did to him," croaks Cycas.

"What does he plan?" Hinoki asks quietly.

"Shen," gasps Cycas.

"Shen, the Dragon of Doom? That cannot be possible," you say. "Shen is only a myth, invented to frighten children."

"Shen will frighten more than children before it is done," whispers Cycas. "It's more than a story. It's real, and it's coming. Zed discovered the spell to call Shen forth. He promised I would be saved. I would have stood at his left hand. I would have been rewarded . . . but the spell was too strong. I wish I could live to see it—the end of the world. . . . "

Suddenly Cycas is seized by a fit of coughing, and as he clutches at your arm, he whispers, "You'll never catch him in time. You're too late—he's gone north to meet the dragon," and dies.

Gently you lower the dead man to the ground. "He must have been delirious. Uncle Zed would never do anything awful like that. What was all that nonsense about the Dragon of Doom?" you ask as you get to your feet.

"No nonsense, I'm afraid. Shen IS the Dragon of Doom. Wherever and whenever he appears, people die. Not just a few, you understand, but lots and lots of people. Whole nations. And not just people. Animals, birds, reptiles, anything that walks, breathes, swims, or flies. If it's alive, it dies."

"I thought that was just a story."

"The council would like to keep it that way,

just a story. A passing dragon told me about
Shen once. Shen used to ravage the earth every
chance that came along, but finally the council
united all the kingdoms and killed all the evil
wizards who knew the spell. Then they burned
every copy of the spell they could find. They
thought it was gone forever and Shen would
sleep for eternity. It appears that your uncle has
rediscovered the spell and called Shen back as
an instrument of revenge."

"I still think this is all ridiculous, but I suppose we'd better do something."

"Like what?" asks Hinoki.

Before deciding, turn to page 25.

1) "Well, I think we should go after Uncle
   Zed and bring him back. Then you'll see
   how wrong you are." If this is your decision, turn to page 143.

2) "We don't know where Zed's gone. We
   might not find him until it's too late. I
   think we should go back to the council and
   let them decide what to do." If this is what
   you decide, turn to page 71.

"This way up. Hmmm . . . well, we fell down for a long time, so I think we should take this door and hope it does go up," you say.

"Your reasoning seems sound," links Hinoki, "and it doesn't seem to be one of Zed's traps. Lead on, Morgan."

The door opens easily to your touch, and you stand in a wide corridor, smoothly paved, with a high ceiling. Soon the path begins to slope up at a steep angle that would be all but impossible to climb. Still a trifle uncertain, you flap your wings and rise straight up into the air. With Hinoki at your side, you follow the shaft, wondering where it will take you.

Your shoulders soon ache with the effort of flying, and still there is no end in sight. The shaft continues on, smooth and seemingly endless. Your muscles burn, and you know you can't possibly last much longer.

"Morgan, you can't stop now," links Hinoki. "You must keep on! To stop would be fatal. If you quit now you would plunge to almost certain death."

"But, Hinoki, I . . . can't . . . go any farther!" you gasp.

"Look ahead of us, Morgan! The tunnel seems to branch off. Can you make it?"

Your mouth is dry and your vision is wobbling, and every last bit of your strength is directed toward keeping yourself aloft. You cannot even answer Hinoki, but you continue to fly as best you can.

"Morgan! Watch out! Your wings aren't flapping in time with each other! You're starting to weave! Morgan! Straighten out! You're going into a spin!"

Concentrating harder than ever before in your life, you try to visualize the wings on your back. Mentally blocking out your pain and exhaustion, you concentrate on breathing smoothly and making your wings operate properly.

As though from a distance, you hear Hinoki say, "Good, Morgan! We're going to make it. Just a little bit farther."

Then suddenly the tunnel ends. You see a room off to one side, with another tunnel leading out of it. You land with a sigh of relief.

Please turn to page 148.

Gradually your eyes adjust to the dim light. You are in a long corridor with high ceilings and stone walls and floor. There are niches in the walls on either side of you, and in the niches are casks and ceramic urns, with gleaming gems and gold coins spilling out of them. At the end of the corridor, you see a large chest. This chest seems to be plain, unornamented wood, and no gems or coins garnish it. There do not appear to be any doors or windows in the corridor.

"What is this place?" you wonder aloud.

"I don't know," links Hinoki curiously. "I'm a stranger here myself."

"What should I do? There doesn't seem to be a way out."

"Oh, I'm sure there's a way out. We just can't see it."

"You mean a trap?"

"Smart boy. You catch on fast."

1) If you want to use the wish ring to see if there are any traps, turn to page 132.

2) If you don't really believe there are any traps and want to check out the treasure chests and urns on the sides of the corridor, turn to page 99.

3) Or if you want to walk down the corridor and examine the plain wooden chest at the end, turn to page 50.

"Look, Morgan. Watch for a minute. There seems to be a pattern to the bubbling," says the little dragon. And through his steady gaze you watch as another bubble grows larger and larger and bursts. You continue to watch as bubble after bubble swells and bursts.

"Hmmm. If we time our approach right, we could probably get through," you murmur. And once more, you and Saffron edge your way out onto the frightening path. Crouching low, the bottoms of your feet growing hotter and hotter, you wait until the next bubble bursts and then race across the rocks.

Just as you reach the far end, Saffron slips and teeters back and forth, trying to catch her balance. You hesitate to touch her for fear of upsetting her balance completely, and you stop breathing until she regains her footing and stands firmly on the rock once again. Although her face is white and pale, she glares at you and says, "Don't just stand there. MOVE!"

In a very short time, you reach the foot of the island. Relief turns to puzzlement as you stare at the sheer black rock that rises straight up out of the sea of lava. Although the path ends at its base, there does not seem to be any way up the slick surface.

"What do we do now?" you wonder aloud.

"Whatever it is, we'll have to do it fast," links Hinoki. "The lava seems to be getting closer."

"It's like a tide, and it's rising. Look," says Saffron.

Turning, you glance down at the long skirt

she holds out for your inspection. To your horror, you see that the edge is singed and steaming. Following her pointing finger, you see that the lava is now nearly to the top of the rock you are standing on. Several rocks are completely buried under the molten mass. It is obvious the level is rising steadily.

1) "Maybe there's still another wish in Zed's ring. We could try to use that." Turn to page 27.

2) "Much as I hate it, I could use the spider climb spell." Turn to page 33.

As the great dragon flies, clouds boil black beneath it, and the land quakes and shudders. Mountain peaks that have stood since time began crumble into adjoining valleys. Long dormant volcanoes spout geysers of lava and poison gas into the air, and terrible storms lash the land.

The dragon ignores the damage, for Shen is the Dragon of Doom. It is only fitting that the land should weep at Shen's passing.

But Shen notes the cold wind upon scales grown thin with age and mourns the loss of his warm, dark cave.

"Who is this mortal who dares to summon me? Why could he not have left me alone? I do not disturb his sleep. Why does he disturb mine? What does he want of me? Wealth? Power? They are all that man ever wants." Forked lightning spews from the dragon's mouth and carves a deep trench in the earth, where nothing will grow for a hundred years.

Slowly, slowly the great dragon flies over the dark edge of the world into the light of day. As the sun caresses its body, Shen's anger lessens. The warmth touches old wounds and hurts and soothes them. It warms Shen's blood, and for a time, the dragon knows peace.

"Perhaps I shall listen to him who has summoned me. Perhaps I shall do his bidding and not eat him directly. I shall see. . . ."

And the Dragon of Doom flies on.

Go back to page 18 and make your decision.

Gathering your wits, you utter the fly spell, and instantly your descent slows.

"Wondered when you'd do that," links Hinoki as he flutters down. "I hope we reach bottom before the spell wears off."

Suddenly you notice something very wrong. Instead of growing feathery wings, you have sprouted dragon wings!

"Hinoki! My spell has gone wrong! What is happening to me?" you shout in alarm.

"Don't worry," links the dragon. "Human spells often work differently here. Be thankful you have those lovely dragon wings. Let's hurry down now before they disappear. You can't tell how long they are going to last."

You are about to answer when a light appears beneath you. You fly down into a large, well lit room. You see a number of skeletons lying about the floor and realize that you were lucky.

There is nothing else in the room except for four doors, each of which has words carved into it. Approaching, you read:

1) "THIS WAY UP." Turn to page 19.

2) "THIS WAY DOWN." Turn to page 130.

3) "THIS WAY OUT." Turn to page 29.

4) "THIS WAY IN." Turn to page 95.

Opening the little leather pouch, you take out the gold band and slip it onto your finger. Once again you marvel as it shrinks to fit your finger. Pointing your hand at the top of the looming stone island, you say, "Magic ring, please take all of us to the top of the island." It seems the words are hardly out of your mouth before you find yourself standing on the top of the island, Saffron at your side.

"Well, now we know that there was at least one wish left," says Hinoki. "If there is another, it's probably the last. But perhaps it was the last."

Please turn to page 118.

Closing your eyes, mind, and heart to the strange girl, you turn away and busy yourself taking off your backpack. Soon the innkeeper returns with a heaped plate of roast lamb, baked new potatoes, and fresh asparagus. You wash it all down with a loaf of crusty bread and several mugs of hot cider. Hinoki allows you to feed him tidbits from your plate. The cider has an odd taste, and soon after you have finished your meal, you begin to grow drowsy.

"Please show me to my room," you say thickly as you struggle to your feet.

"Yes, sir, but the creature cannot go with you. It will have to sleep in the barn," the innkeeper says nervously. "We don't allow animals in the rooms."

"I don't think that's wise," Hinoki's voice mind-links. "Tell him no. He's up to no good."

1) If you think you should refuse to let Hinoki sleep in the barn, tell the innkeeper no and turn to page 87.

2) If you are too sleepy to argue, tell Hinoki to sleep in the barn and turn to page 100.

"Morgan, this couldn't be a door for dragons. It's too small."

"You're a dragon and you're fitting through it," you say as you open the door and walk through.

"Yes . . . well, sort of. I mean, not really."

Amazed, you turn around and look at him. "What do you mean, 'sort of, not really'?"

"Well, lots of people don't consider pseudo-dragons to be dragons. That's why we're called pseudo, or false, dragons. Some dragons even pretend they can't see us and won't talk to us."

"That's nonsense. As far as I'm concerned, you're real and you fit through the door, so I'm sure it's going to be all right. So hurry up."

"But, Morgan, look at this fog. I can't even see where I'm going. How can I go faster? I can hardly see in front of my beak."

"Sit on my shoulder then. I'll keep my hands stretched out in front of me so we won't bump into anything."

You feel a nagging doubt in the back of your mind that maybe you should have listened to Hinoki, but you brush it aside and fly. From time to time, the fog parts and you see that you are in a rough stone tunnel with high ceilings and a dirt floor. Then the fog closes about you thicker than ever, and you see nothing. The hair on the back of your neck begins to crinkle and you slow almost to a halt.

"What's the matter," links Hinoki.

"I don't know, but something's wrong. I can feel it." Slowly you fly forward, fingers out-

stretched, groping. Then, to your horror, you feel something soft and furry . . . something that moves!

The fog parts and there, under your finger-tips, you see an enormous shaggy pelt wrapped around an even more enormous belly. You raise your eyes, and there, looming high above you, is the biggest, ugliest, most muscular giant you have ever seen in your life.

Grinning, he raises what looks like a full-grown oak trunk and swings it at you.

Clutching Hinoki to your chest, you take one last look at the awful face before the fog blots it from view, then fly down the tunnel as fast as you can. A powerful burst of air rushes past your face as the giant's club thuds into the ground next to you.

"Come back! I squash you flat!" roars the giant.

Suddenly, without any warning, you crash full into a bend in the tunnel and fall stunned upon the ground.

"I got you now! I squash you good!" bellows the giant, and a brief parting of the mist reveals the giant straddling your body, club raised on high. As you raise yourself groggily on one elbow, you see the club begin its whistling descent, and darkness engulfs you.

THE END

"I am weary," the mighty Shen thinks as it forces its great wings to lift for yet another beat. "I am tired of man and his petty battles. His greed for gems and other treasure is not for the beauty they contain but for his own selfish interests.

"Man knows nothing of the secrets contained in the heart of a ruby, the mind of an emerald, or the eye of a sapphire. He is too busy killing and destroying.

"Perhaps man has been a mistake. Maybe it is best that he disappear from the face of the earth once and for all. Then dragons and other creatures of beauty may live in peace.

"I will answer this summons. Perhaps I am wrong. Perhaps man is not all bad. I will decide what must be done when I get there."

And the great dragon flies on, though its wings ache with the effort and it longs for its beautiful, warm cave.

Far below, the clouds boil and spew hot rain that weeps upon the cowering earth. Soon trees and grasslands give way to empty lands where there is nothing but rocks. The air grows hot, and far below, the dragon sees a sea of lava lapping at the land. "Ahh, the End of the World," sighs the dragon, and it begins to descend.

Please turn to page 35.

"I've always hated this spell," you say, pulling out a tiny vial and a small round box.

"Why?" asks Saffron as she stands on tiptoe and looks anxiously at the rising lava.

Shuddering, you uncork the vial and drink the potion it contains. Then, fighting a surge of distaste, you take the lid off the box, reach inside, grab the wriggling spider it contains, and swallow the spider whole.

"You're not supposed to SWALLOW it," lectures Hinoki. "You're supposed to EAT it."

"If you want to eat a spider, you do it," you choke. "It's all I can do just to swallow the cursed things. I hate doing that."

"Just imagine how THEY feel," says Hinoki.

"I can't believe you just did that," says Saffron, staring at you with her big blue eyes.

"Good grief!" you sigh. "It's bad enough having to do this, without your comments. Saffron, unless you want to turn into a cinder, get over here and put your arms around my neck."

"Why?" Saffron asks suspiciously.

"Because it's the only way we're going to get out of here alive!"

With a last look at the rapidly advancing lava, Saffron picks up her skirts, moves over beside you, and wraps both arms around your neck.

"Don't let go, whatever you do," you caution. Then, turning to the glassy rock face, you place both hands and a foot upon the slick surface. You feel the slippery surface taking on a new character under your sensitive fingertips. Tiny cracks and crevices you cannot even see reveal themselves to your feet and hands. As surely as if you were walking on a level surface, you scramble up the side of the cliff.

Hinoki circles above you, lending encouragement, but Saffron hangs from your throat, threatening to pull you from your hold by her weight. To make matters worse, Grundoon, back inside Saffron's pack again, keeps bumping your legs, threatening to trip you.

"Put your arms around my shoulders, not my neck!" you croak as your breath grows short.

Abruptly the pressure eases as Saffron transfers her grip to your shoulders and wraps her legs around your waist. With great relief, you quickly scramble the rest of the way up the side of the cliff and finally crawl over the edge.

With a deep sigh, you collapse on the flat surface and try to regain your breath.

Please turn to page 118.

It seems as if you have been walking forever. The swamp is now far behind you, and a thick mist wraps itself around you. From time to time, you feel the ground rumble beneath you. Jets of hot gas fill the air with the stench of hot metal.

"I don't like the looks of this," Saffron says, trembling.

"Neither do I, but we have to go on. I'm sure Zed's not far from here."

"Hinoki, let's try scanning and see if we can find him. Saffron can help us and we'll be able to see even better."

"How do you do this 'scanning'?" asks Saffron, moving to your side.

"It's similar to what we did when we healed the couatl. Just fix your thoughts on Hinoki, and you can see whatever he sees."

You both sit down on a rock outcrop and look at the pseudo-dragon. "Now cast your mind into his. Become one with him."

Gently, like remembering a favorite daydream, you slip into Hinoki's mind. Suddenly you are viewing yourself sitting on the rock, through Hinoki's eyes.

"It feels weird—sort of like I'm sleeping or dreaming," Saffron says.

Spreading his wings, Hinoki flaps up into the mist, and you see your body grow small.

"I'm getting dizzy," gulps Saffron.

"It does that to me, too. Try not to think about it. It's okay unless he dives suddenly. Will you look at that!"

Below your view, the mists swirl as though

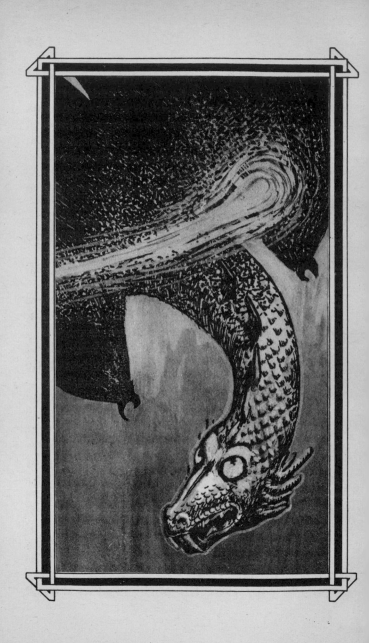

directed by a million currents. Plumes of steam burst from the ground. Here and there, geysers of molten rock spew into the air.

"I don't see how we'll find anybody here," links Hinoki. "An army could hide in those mists and we wouldn't see them."

"Saffron, let's try listening for Zed. Maybe we can hear his thoughts even if we can't see him. With three of us, we ought to have a pretty good range."

As the frightening landscape slides beneath you, you search off to Hinoki's left and feel nothing. You repeat the process straight ahead, again without success.

Finally, as you focus to Hinoki's right, a dry, cracked voice slides into your mind. Concentrating deeply, you find you can make out snatches of words: ". . . should be here soon . . . know he'll grant my wish . . . cannot refuse me . . . all the treasure in the world . . . all my enemies dead . . . the hour approaches . . . revenge will be mine. I'll teach them to— Eh! Who's there?"

Abruptly, the voice disappears as though it never existed.

"Get down!" you yell, and Hinoki drops like a stone as a blue bolt of energy sizzles through the air and explodes above him.

"What was that?" gasps Saffron.

"A mind missile—a really high-level spell that magic-users can use against anyone who tries to probe their minds. I was afraid he'd do that. Well, now we know he's here. Unfortunately, he knows we're here, too, and from what he said, there isn't too much time."

All day long you push on through the frightening landscape. The smoke and heat and fiery explosions seem to be getting worse. The ground continues to shake almost without pause.

"Stop!" commands Hinoki. "There's nothing in front of us but air!"

Dropping to your knees, you place your hands on the hot ground and slowly crawl forward, peering into the billowing black smoke.

"Do you see anything, Morgan?" Saffron asks.

Before you can answer, the ground gives way abruptly beneath your probing fingers, and you fall flat on your face. As you lie with your cheek pressed against the burning earth, the smoke parts for a second and you see an amazing sight. Before you lies an immense hole in the earth. Deeper and wider than you can guess, it stretches off into the distance.

Directly beneath you, you spot a narrow ledge that leads down into the dizzying depths. Far, far below, you see an orange glow. Through narrowed eyes, you are able to make out a narrow path leading through the burning landscape toward what appears to be a flat-topped rock rising out of the pit.

Crawling back from the edge of the pit, you report what you have seen.

"Do you think that's where Zed is headed?" asks Saffron with a shiver.

"I'm sure of it. As much as I'd like to believe otherwise, in my heart I know that's where he's

going. We'll be right behind him."

"What is your plan, Morgan?" links Hinoki.

"I—I think we should leave," says Saffron. "I don't want any part of this."

"I have a mission, Saffron. I can't stop now, and neither can you. You'd never find your way out of here alone. And, besides, unless we stop Zed, there might not even be a world left for you to return to."

"You don't know that for sure," Saffron says fearfully.

"No, I don't," you answer. "But I have a pretty good idea, and so do you."

"Saffron," links Hinoki. "Zed is much more powerful than we are. Alone, we have little or no chance of success. The only people who are strong enough to stop him are far from here. If the world is to be saved, I'm afraid we'll have to do it together. I can't promise we'll live through it, but we must try—and you must help us."

"But I'm frightened," whispers Saffron. "Besides, the world has never done anything good for me."

"You can't blame the world for the misfortunes that life has dealt you," links Hinoki. "It owes you nothing. You have been given the precious gift of life, and that is all that anyone can ask. It is up to you what you make of your life. Don't waste it blaming others for your problems. If you want something, you must make it happen yourself. You can count on no one but yourself in the long run."

"If that's true, why should I help you?" asks

Saffron, confused.

"Because some things are more important than self. This is one of them."

"And also because we're your friends and we need you," you add.

"I'll come," Saffron says, looking ashamed. "I have nothing to go back to. You're my only friends besides Grundoon. What do you want me to do? I don't have much experience with this end-of-the-world stuff."

"Neither do I. We'll just have to take it a step at a time," you answer. "You'd better put that cat of yours in your backpack, or he'll just be in the way."

Carefully you scout the edge of the inferno. Taking a deep breath, you lead the way down the trail that snakes its way down the inside face of the cauldron in a snarl of sharp rocks.

You see Saffron tremble as she clings to the rough rock. Your stomach heaves as you look down at the boiling mass below you, and words of comfort die on your lips.

"I'll scan ahead, so you know what to expect," links Hinoki, and with a rush of wings, he's gone. Fearfully you enter his mind and watch as the path unfolds before his eyes. Hot currents buffet the small dragon, flinging him up and down and threatening to crush him against the wall. Slowly you progress, clutching Saffron's hand as though it were a lifeline.

Foot by dangerous foot, you inch your way down the treacherous trail. As you descend, the heat steadily grows more intense. Finally you are able to see the floor of the inferno all too clearly. Fear fills you as you realize that the red glow is molten lava seething restlessly under a thin crust. As you watch, the surface heaves up and down as though swelled by a great tide.

At long last, you reach the bottom of the trail. From close up, the vast sea of molten lava is even more terrifying than it was at a distance. Hissing and steaming constantly, it flings itself against the cliff like waves upon the shore. Your destination, the rock island you saw from above, is lost from sight in the rising steam of the inferno.

"Where do we go from here?" Saffron asks in a small voice.

"I see rocks over to the left," links Hinoki. "And I see what could be a trail leading to the island. It looks dangerous, but I think you can do it." Through his eyes, you see the rocks, narrow and drenched with lava spray, stretching off into the distance.

"Morgan, I don't think I can do it. What if I slip? What if we fall?" Saffron says.

"It's no good thinking about it, Saffron. It's not going to get any better."

Clutching her hand in yours, you make your way down the final stretch. Despite the intense heat, you take your cloak out of your pack and put it on.

"Put yours on, too, Saffron. If the spray hits you, the cloak might protect you."

Finally reaching the bottom of the pit, you step gingerly out onto the first stone. It burns the soles of your feet, but you find that if you keep moving, the heat is bearable. Just as you begin to feel that crossing the lava pool may be easier than you thought, Hinoki's voice bursts inside your mind. "Look there! Watch out, Morgan!"

Images flood your mind and you are able to see through Hinoki's eyes as an enormous lava bubble swells above the surface just a short distance from where you stand.

"Run!" screams Hinoki as the bubble grows larger and larger.

Pushing Saffron before you, you turn around and race back over the stepping-stones. Reaching the edge of the pool, you fling yourself behind an outcropping of rocks just as the now enormous bubble bursts, showering the nearby rocks with molten lava.

Grundoon, trapped inside Saffron's backpack, yowls in fear and claws frantically at the stiff material.

"Do you really think we can do it?" asks Saffron, poking her finger through a charred hole in her cloak.

"We've got to," you say.

Please turn to page 23.

"I suppose you think that men are too greedy because they're always trying to steal your treasure," you say. "That makes sense. I think greed is the right answer."

"Wrong!" bellows the dragon, breathing a cloud of black smoke over you. As you and Hinoki grow smaller and smaller, you hear the dragon say, "Man has MORE than enough greed! He doesn't need any more!"

"Wait! You tricked me!" you holler in a tiny voice. "That's not fair!"

"Who ever said I would be fair?" answers the dragon. And as you press your nose against the glass and stare out at it, the dragon laughs and laughs and laughs.

THE END

Hurriedly you plunge your hand in your pocket and wriggle the wish ring over your finger. "Oh, please, magic ring, if you've ever worked before, work now! Please give me wings, and I promise I'll be good for the rest of my life!"

For a moment, nothing happens. Then you begin to feel a tingle between your shoulder blades. No, it's not a tingle. It's more like an itch—the kind you can never quite reach. As you tumble through the air, you reach back frantically and try to scratch the cursed itch.

Your fingers brush against something, something odd. Puzzled, you try to turn to look. You spin round and round in midair, trying to catch a good look at whatever it is, but no matter how fast you turn, it seems to turn as quickly as you do.

"You look very silly doing that," links Hinoki as he flutters down and hovers before your face. "What are you doing?"

"Trying to see what that is behind me!" you gasp indignantly.

"Those? Those are your wings. You remember—the wings you promised to be good for the rest of your life for," answers Hinoki amusedly.

"It is? They ARE? Oh! I really have them?"

"How else do you suppose you've been floating around talking to me?" asks Hinoki.

"Floating? Flying? ME? Oh!" you say, and as you look down at the void beneath you, you panic and begin to fall again.

"Help! Help!"

"Morgan, calm down! You don't need anyone to help you. Help yourself," links Hinoki. "Use your wings!"

Desperately you try flapping your new appendages. Immediately you stop falling and lurch drunkenly to the side. You try to correct and find yourself falling off to the other side.

"No, no! You've got it all wrong!" nags Hinoki. "Do it like this."

Fearfully you try to imitate his motions, until at last you are fluttering and flying and swooping and diving with confidence.

"This is fantastic! This is wonderful! Why didn't you tell me it was so much fun?"

"Don't be silly," links Hinoki. "When's the last time you told me how much fun it is to walk or swim? Nonetheless, I'm glad you're enjoying it so much. It will make your promise less difficult to keep."

"What promise?"

"The promise to be good for the rest of your life. Remember?"

And with a groan, you remember your promise. Sighing deeply, you circle, then dive for the bottom of the trap.

Please turn to page 148.

"Quick, Saffron, give me your food sack," you whisper as you clutch your bag of rations.

"Why?" asks Saffron as she passes you the bag.

"The hydra's hungry. It doesn't care what it eats. Maybe it'll settle for this instead of us." You pull out a large round of cheese and throw it into the air, directly in front of the hydra head hovering above you.

The hydra watches the cheese until it reaches its highest point, then plucks it out of the air and swallows it whole.

"It might work," whispers Hinoki. "Try the same thing on some of the other heads."

Putting all your power into the throw, you arc a smoked ham just past the nearest hydra head. The hydra snaps wildly at the ham but misses. Roaring angrily, it goes after the ham, snuffling in the water where it sank.

Two of the other heads join the first head in the search. Soon the three heads are fighting among themselves, snatching and tearing at the hunk of meat. Two of its remaining heads seem to have decided that you are probably tastier than the ham and are approaching rapidly. The last head snaps futilely at Hinoki, who hovers just out of its reach.

Scrambling to your knees, you grab Saffron's hand tightly and then throw two cheeses and a loaf of black bread off to one side. Instantly the two heads that were advancing toward you dive for the food, jerking the other heads with them.

As fast as you are able, you slosh off into the

swamp, away from the terrible six-headed monster.

As you round a small clump of trees, you steal one last backward glance. All six heads of the hydra are snarling and snapping at each other as they fight over the food.

"I never thought we'd get out of that alive," Saffron sighs, wiping her eyes.

Knees shaking, you sink down on a mudbank and nod in agreement.

Please turn to page 32.

"I'll bet this is a test, Hinoki," you link. "Maybe we're supposed to pick the plain chest over the ones with the treasure to show we're not greedy. Or maybe we're supposed to think that's the answer, and there's a trap still waiting for us."

"Just be careful, Morgan. There's no way we can think of all the angles. You can second guess until you're blue in the face and still never be sure."

Holding your breath, you walk down the corridor, sliding one foot after the other. At one point, a small dragonne, sleeping unseen in a chest, explodes into the air and flies off. Startled, you step aside, and for a moment, the floor seems to tilt under your feet. But then you regain your balance, and the floor seems steady again.

"Did I imagine that?" you ask Hinoki.

"I don't know, but don't do it again," links the little dragon.

Finally you reach the end of the long corridor and stand in front of the wooden chest, wondering if you have chosen correctly.

"It doesn't look like much, does it?"

"You never can tell about these things, Morgan. Remember, things are not always what they appear," Hinoki says.

You stare at the chest for a long time but avoid touching it. It is quite large, probably big enough to hold six people with room left over. Constructed of plain, unpainted wood, it is bound on all four edges with black iron. A large iron hasp holds it shut. There is no lock.

Summoning your courage, you peer behind it. It seems to be no more and no less than it appears—a simple chest.

"What should I do?" you wonder aloud.

1) "We could try to open the chest." Turn to page 137.

2) "Or we can forget about it and look at those jeweled chests." Turn to page 99.

"Perhaps you are my nephew after all," says Zed. Holding your chin in his bony fingers, his black eyes look deep into yours. You feel a chill pass through you at his touch.

Then the chill becomes a current of coldness, enveloping you in its icy grip. Inside your head, Hinoki screams a warning, and vaguely you feel Saffron tugging at your arm, but it doesn't matter. Nothing matters. The coldness surges through you until you feel it creeping into your very soul. When Zed releases you at last, you feel changed somehow. But you were tired of that self, always so good, so obedient, so boring.

You feel a new strength flood your body, but a slight uneasiness nibbles at you, and you pause briefly. Then your uncle takes you by the arm and says, "Come! The hour of our destiny is upon us!"

Looking up into the howling sky, you see a black speck high above you. As you stare, it grows larger and larger.

"Hang on, Morgan! Don't give in! We'll save you somehow!" cries Hinoki's voice inside your head. But you close your mind and continue to stare, entranced.

The sky is filled with streaks of lightning. The wind screams about your ears, adding its wild keening to your uncle's crazed laughter. You are confused and frightened, but you are strangely excited. You are not sure if this is the beginning or . . .

THE END

The rest of the day passes without incident, and evening finds you deep within the heart of the swamp.

"I think we should stop here for the evening," you say. And though your muscles ache, you gather dry twigs and grasses and build a fire. Grateful for its warmth, you sink down on a moss-covered log. The log settles under your weight, and you sit wearily, with your head in your hands.

Beneath you, you feel the log move again. Just as you are beginning to wonder why, you notice that there is a long, snaky vine wrapped around your ankle. As you reach down to take it off, another vine slithers out of the ooze and wraps itself firmly around your other leg.

"Great. Now I'm being attacked by vines!" you say with a sigh. As you try to untangle it, you slip your hand under the vine, and suddenly it tightens. You find it impossible to withdraw your hand. You feel terribly silly, sitting all bent over, wrapped in vines. As you sit tugging at your hand, trying to figure out what to do, something soft but heavy clouts you on the head, and the world spins before your eyes. "HELLPPP!" you cry. Silly or not, you need someone to come to your aid.

"It's a shambler!" shrieks Saffron as she rushes in carrying a load of firewood. "Do something, Morgan!"

"What do you mean, DO something! A vegetable is trying to eat me, and you say DO something! YOU do something!"

"Shambling mounds aren't vegetables," Saffron sniffs as she whacks the log with a stout stick. "They only look like logs, but they're alive, and they can think, and they can kill you."

"Don't give me a lecture! Just help me! Ouch! Watch out! You just hit me!"

1) "I'll kill it with my knife," says Saffron as she draws a glistening blade. Turn to page 129.

2) "Fire! Try to burn it up!" shouts Hinoki. Turn to page 110.

3) "Wait! Let me try a charm plant spell!" you cry. Turn to page 124.

The rocks are rough and tear your hands badly, and the wind does its best to rip you off the face of the wall. It is not safe to use your wings, but with more than your share of luck, you are able to climb to the bottom of the long, dark pit.

Clinging to the wall, you peer at the bottom of the pit. You see a faint light around its edges, but nothing else. Maybe if you get close, you'll be able to see a little better.

"What do you see, Morgan?" links Hinoki.

"Nothing. The light down here isn't so good. I think I'm going to walk out to the center. It seems solid." And brushing Hinoki's objections aside, you step out onto the dark floor.

Instantly the downdraft slams into you, the floor drops away, and you fall, with Hinoki's cries of distress ringing in your ears. You land heavily on your shoulder and lie stunned, with all the breath knocked out of you.

"Get up!" commands a harsh voice.

Peering upward, you see a medium-size dragon standing over you.

"Get up, man person! It is time for you to die!" snarls the dragon as a flow of flames from its nostrils sears your leg.

"Die? Why?" you say, scooting backward on a hard dirt surface.

"Because those are the rules here in the pit. He who is unfortunate enough to fall into it must wait until another suffers the same fate. Then it is a fight to the finish. Only one may survive in the pit," hisses the dragon as it advances.

"What happens if no one falls in?" you ask, crawling faster.

"Then you die anyway," says the dragon, kicking a skeleton aside.

"B-But wait," you say as you back into the stone wall circling the pit. "What happens if you fight and win?"

"I don't know," says the dragon, smiling as he closes in for the kill. "But I intend to find out."

THE END

Keeping a sharp eye out for shambling mounds or any other monsters, you get an early start and soon find yourselves winding deeper and deeper into the gloomy swamp, now covered by a thick layer of mist.

"Grundoon! No, Grundoon! Come back!" screams Saffron suddenly. You see an orange blur, and the cat leaps onto a mudbank and disappears in a swirl of mist.

"Please—please help me catch him," sobs Saffron.

"How? I can barely see my hand in front of my face in this fog. Besides, I don't think he wants to be caught. He jumped of his own accord. Let him stay here."

"PLEASE don't leave him! I've had him since he was just a little kitten, and he—he means a lot to me," begs Saffron.

"All right! All right!" you sigh. "I know I'll regret this, but I'll do it."

Slogging through the misty gloom, you call, "Here, kitty, kitty, kitty! Here, Grundoon!"

"Meow! Meow! Meowr!"

"He's over there—off to the left!" you call, changing direction.

"MEOWWW!"

"Grundoon! Hurry, Morgan! Something's happened!" cries Saffron.

"Blasted cat! Serve it right if something ate it!" you mutter as you trudge through the knee-high water. "Here, kitty, kitty, kitty!"

"Hiss! Hiss! Rowrrr!"

"There you are you, little cannibal! Why are

you all fluffed up like that? I'm not going to hurt you," you say.

As you slide your hand under Grundoon's stomach, the cat gives a wild shriek, races up your arm, and tries to burrow under Hinoki.

"Now you've done it! Look! I'm bleeding," you say as you hold up your scratched hand. Suddenly something moves. Perhaps it was the mist, or maybe your eyes are playing tricks on you, but it seemed that you saw something—something big!

"It was no trick. I saw it, too," links Hinoki. "Try moving away quietly. Maybe it hasn't seen us yet, whatever it is."

"Morgan! Grundoon!" calls Saffron. "Oh, there you are, Morgan. Have you found him?" Saffron asks breathlessly. . . . "Oh, you have. Grundoon, you're so bad!" And reaching over, she draws the cat toward her, ignoring its angry squawls and wildly flailing claws.

Clutching your scratched neck, you open your mouth to speak, but your mouth remains open and you say nothing.

"Morgan, why are you staring like that? You really look quite silly!"

But you do not answer. All you can do is stare upward at an enormous reptilian head staring down at you through the mist. Then, even as you notice the tiny cold eyes and the mouth full of sharp teeth gaping toward you, you see yet another head, and another, and another!

"Morgan, it's a hydra!" links Hinoki excitedly.

"What are you two talking about?" asks Saffron as she struggles with the panic-stricken cat.

"Oh!" she gasps as she looks up. "I see!"

Gathering your courage, you make your decision and say:

1) "Maybe I can fight it." If this is what you decide, turn to page 140.

2) "Maybe it hasn't seen us yet and we can run away." If this is your decision, turn to page 77.

3) "Maybe I can use Zed's ring of wishes." If you want to use the ring, turn to page 97.

4) "Maybe I can trick it." If you think you can trick the hydra, turn to page 48.

"What do we do now, Hinoki," you link nervously.

"Well, there's no sense going back the way we came, so I suggest we go forward," answers the preudo-dragon.

Laboriously you trudge through the treasure, which sucks at your legs. Your legs ache with weariness. Suddenly you find yourself facing two huge black pillars that frame an immense door, covered with black diamonds.

Slowly you approach the door. Much to your amazement, it swings open silently at your touch. The treasure is piled even thicker underfoot, but you scarcely notice it. What you do notice is the huge throne rising from the center of the room.

You climb a small mountain of treasure and gaze at the throne in awe. Solid black, it gleams with a radiance that almost seems alive. Touching it, you are not surprised to find that it is warm.

"It's a dragon throne," links Hinoki. "Look how big it is. I can't even imagine a dragon that big!"

Your attention is drawn to a great globe balanced by the side of the throne. Twice as tall as you are, the black glass globe seems to contain some form of life. Deep within, you see a swirl of movement. Puzzled, you move closer and peer into its depths. Black mists swirl, and as they part for an instant, you see a face—a human face! The mouth opens and screams soundlessly. Hands reach out for help. And then the figure is gone, swallowed by the mists.

As you watch in horror, other faces appear and disappear inside the globe. All beg silently for help.

"Hinoki, what is this thing? Who are these people! We've got to get them out!"

"It's obviously a magic device that belongs to whomever sits on this throne," answers Hinoki. "I don't know who these people are, but I wouldn't free them if I were you. The dragon must want them there."

"But they're people! I can't just leave them there like fish in a bowl! Think how we'd feel if we were trapped in there!"

Before Hinoki can reply, you pick up a half-buried sword and strike the globe a mighty blow. Instantly the glass shatters into a million fragments, and black smoke swirls out into the room. Tiny figures, no bigger than your little fingernail, tumble out at your feet. As the air washes away the smoke, the figures begin to grow. Larger and larger they become, until they stand about you in a great crowd.

"Wh-who are you, and what were you doing in that globe?" you stammer, staring at the warriors who surround you.

"We are adventurers," answers an old man clad in full armor. "We all came seeking the dragon's treasure. And one by one, we all were trapped inside that globe till you set us free. How were you able to do this? Is the Great Dragon dead?"

"I—I don't know. I don't even know which

dragon you speak of."

At your words, the warriors clutch their weapons and stare about fearfully. Then, one by one, they hurry away in terror.

"Wait! Don't go!" you cry, but your words are all but drowned out by a great rush of wind that beats down on you from above.

Only the old man remains. "Hurry or we die!" he pleads, tugging at your arm.

"I cannot leave!" you say, and with a frantic cry, the man hurries after the others.

Sinking to your knees, you press against the black throne and look up. Diving straight down toward you, claws extended, is a massive silver dragon! You heart skips a beat and you are faint with fear.

"Courage, Morgan!" links Hinoki. "Remember your mission!"

As the great dragon settles into the seat of its throne and fixes you with a steely glare, you try to do as Hinoki suggested. Standing tall with a courage you do not really feel, you face the throne. Bowing low, you say, "Greetings, Great Dragon. I am Morgan, son of Ethelred, nephew of Zed, and messenger of the Council of Nine. I am here on a mission."

The dragon blinks when you mention your uncle. Then, its black tongue flickering, it hisses, "Was it part of your mission to break my globe?"

"I'm sorry about that," you say, returning its gaze calmly. "But I could not leave the warriors trapped inside."

"It is no matter," says the dragon. "I can make another." And pointing its long, metallic snout over the edge of the throne, it blows a stream of silvery black smoke. The smoke forms into a round shape, then somehow crystallizes, and before you, resting atop the pile of treasure, is another glass globe.

"It will fill quickly," says the dragon, smiling evilly. "And you will be its first occupant, unless you can answer the riddle."

"What riddle?" you ask fearfully.

"This one," smirks the dragon, and coiling its long metallic body, it settles comfortably before it speaks.

"What does man possess but never have enough of, and once he gains it, it only increases his desire for more?"

"Why should I play your game? You'll probably put me in that globe or eat me no matter how I answer. If I answer correctly, will you assist me in my mission?"

"Why should I do that—even assuming that you could answer the riddle correctly, which you can't?" says the dragon.

"Because dragons are supposed to be honorable," says Hinoki. "If he is willing to play your game and abide by your rules, then you should be willing to abide by his terms if you lose."

"I lose? I will never lose!" laughs the dragon. "What have I to fear of your silly terms? But you will not win, not even if I give you a hint. Not even if I give you the answers!" A smile plays across the dragon's lips. Its tail digs into the treasure and flips a gold coin into the air play-fully.

As your eyes follow the coin, the dragon says, "Here, young man—here are the answers. Choose wisely!"

1) "Greed." If you think this is the correct answer to the riddle, turn to page 44.

2) "Love of gold." If you think this is the proper choice, turn to page 78.

3) "I don't like either of those choices," you say. "My answer is love." If this is your answer, turn to page 113.

"I'm sorry, but we can't possibly help you," you say. "We're trying to stop this man ourselves. If we stay, we'll lose time. When we get to the next town, I'll send someone for you."

The couatl looks at you through its silver eyes and groans pitifully.

"That stinks!" shouts Saffron. "I'm not going anywhere with you! You can send someone back for me and Grundoon, too!"

"That's fine!" you shout back. "I never asked you to come in the first place!" You turn and stare angrily at Hinoki. "I suppose you agree! Well, you can stay here, too. I don't need any of you." And thrusting Hinoki into Saffron's hands, you stomp off into the swamp.

Hours later, you are beginning to regret your hasty words and terrible temper. You wish the others were with you—even Grundoon. Finally you decide to return and apologize.

You turn around to start back, but one leg sinks to the knees in the mud. You try to pull it out, but it sinks deeper. You search for something to cling to, but there is nothing.

In desperation, you throw a rope around a nearby tree. It catches, but as you tug, the branch breaks. Soon you have sunk nearly to your chest. Struggling only makes it worse, so you cease to struggle and think about what a fool you have been. If only you hadn't lost your temper. If only you had helped the couatl. If only it weren't . . .

THE END

Angrily you stomp out of the inn into the cold and gusty night. Pulling your cloak around you, you manage to find shelter under the branches of a great cedar tree. Sleep is difficult. Although the rain cannot get you, the cold wind does, and the ground is cold and hard.

"Stop complaining," links Hinoki. "Your thoughts are keeping me awake." Then, tucking his head under his wing, he goes to sleep.

Suddenly a small furry figure leaps upon your leg. You feel sharp claws dig into your flesh. Shrieking with the unexpected pain, you leap to your feet, bumping your head on a cedar branch. Hinoki topples off your shoulder and clutches at you with his razor-sharp claws. Meanwhile, the small creature clings to your leg, biting ferociously.

"Grundoon, don't be naughty," says a soft voice, and then, miraculously, the beast, which you now see is only a large orange cat, is removed from your leg. Scooping up the struggling pseudo-dragon, you part the branches and look out into the eyes of the girl from the inn.

"You! What are you doing here? Haven't you caused enough trouble for one night? If it weren't for you, I'd be sleeping in a warm bed right now!" you sputter.

"And likely be dead," answers the girl. "Yesterday a strange man, the one you seek, passed through here. He made my master promise that he would prevent anyone from following him. You must leave now. It is not safe, even here. My master is searching for you at this very

moment. When he finds you, he will kill you."

"But why should he want to kill me? He doesn't even know me. And if he's looking for me, how is it that you could find me and he couldn't? Are you trying to kill us?" you ask as your hand tightens about your staff.

"The old man promised to come back and kill my master if he did not do his bidding. He killed my master's dog just by looking at it. I found you by following your thoughts—they were very loud—and I don't want to kill you. In fact, I have come to beg you to take me with you. I can follow the old man you seek through his thoughts. I can be of great help. I want to leave here. Please take me with you!"

Please turn to page 92.

As you stand before the council, you can't help feeling that you have failed. "If only . . ." you are thinking, but then elder Fazad speaks.

"We must find Zed before he does something foolish."

"I cannot believe he would end the world," says the Baron Beta, shaking his head.

"We cannot take the chance," intones Fazad. "Morgan, you must find your uncle and bring him back. If you cannot bring him back, you must stop him from doing any damage."

"Gladly, sir, but how? I do not know where to find him. If he's to meet the Dragon of Doom, the meeting must be in a secret place. I don't know where that place is. Do you?"

The gray heads of the Council of Nine shake from side to side, and only silence meets your question. The silence lengthens to long moments as the old ones stare at each other in despair.

"I know where he'll be," Hinoki says quietly.

"YOU!" snorts the Baron Beta. "How would you know?"

"I, sir, am a dragon. And all dragons, large or small, know where the meeting place is."

"Tell us!" demands Beta, leaning forward in his chair.

"I cannot do that, sir. My allegiance is to Morgan. If Morgan wishes to accompany me, I will take him, but I cannot tell you."

"We should have cracked his shell when he was still in the egg," mutters another council member.

"Please! Please! No more quarreling," begs Fazad, holding up his frail hands. "Hinoki, if you know where this meeting is to take place, please take Morgan there. You do not need to tell us where it is. If you succeed, well and good. If you do not . . . well, then, it will be too late for us to do anything, even if we know where the meeting is to take place. So go. Do your best. Our hopes and our prayers are with you."

Bowing low, you back out of the council chambers, with Hinoki sitting firmly on your shoulder.

"I can see why your uncle wouldn't want to come back. What a bunch of prunes!" links Hinoki, once you are outside.

"They're not prunes," you say, your voice quavering. "They're just old and careful."

"What's the matter? Why are you sad?" Hinoki links, rubbing his head up and down against your ear. When you do not answer, he stretches his neck and peers upside down into your face. He looks so silly that, in spite of yourself, you have to laugh.

Hugging the small dragon to your chest, you sit up with a sigh and say, "I just don't understand why you had to go and tell them that you know where he's going! How are we going to get out of this now?"

"But I DO know where he's going," links Hinoki, grooming his silver scales with his little red forked tongue.

"You really do? You weren't just showing off?" you yell, jumping to your feet.

"Of course I do," says Hinoki, scrambling to regain his balance. "Would I fool you?"

"Well, there was that time you woke me in the middle of the night and told me there was a tornado, and I ran outside without any clothes on."

"Oh, that! That was just a joke."

"And this?" you demand.

"This is no joke. I really do know where they're going. You'll just have to trust me."

You remember little of the difficult journey that follows except for long, twisting mountain trails and tired, aching muscles. Hinoki blindfolds you for the last part of the trip, and soon after, you feel the damp coolness of what must be a secret tunnel. Finally you emerge, and Hinoki removes your blindfold.

"Ahh, doesn't it feel wonderful?" links Hinoki as he stretches his little wings and cranes his neck up toward the sun.

Blinking, you look around in confusion. "Where are we? What is this place?"

"It's a place that all dragon's know about," answers Hinoki. "If they're sick or old or simply wish to hatch their eggs in safety, they can come here. Man is not welcome."

"Then, then what about me?" you ask in panic, clutching your dagger.

"There are exceptions, of course. Some of us are linked to men, and if we bring you here, you are safe from harm unless you do something to betray our friendship. Then neither of us would live. But, of course, I know you would never do that. Now, put that dagger away before you get us both in real trouble."

Somewhat reassured, you put your dagger back in its sheath and look about curiously.

You are in a field filled with flowers and high grasses. Large boulders dot the field, and on almost every boulder is a dragon, sunning itself. You eye the long grass nervously, realizing that it could easily hide a small dragon. You finger your dagger thoughtfully.

"As long as you act honorably, you are completely safe," links Hinoki. "Try to forget that you are a man and have this uncontrollable urge to kill dragons just to prove how brave you are."

"But dragons are dangerous!" you protest. "If we didn't kill them, they'd kill us!"

"Most dragons want nothing more than to be left in peace," snaps Hinoki. "A long time ago, men and dragons lived in peace together, but then man got greedy and invented something called chivalry as an excuse to kill dragons and take their treasure. It works pretty well for man, but not so well for dragons."

"Um, why don't we continue this discussion later? Maybe we should get on with our mission," you say.

"Yes, maybe we should," Hinoki snaps testily and takes his place on your shoulder.

"Which way do we go?" you ask politely.

"Straight ahead to the castle," Hinoki answers.

Although you see no castle, you begin to walk straight ahead. You try not to think of all the things the long grass brushing against you might conceal. Your path takes you past a great gray rock. On top of the rock is an enormous dragon with a half-healed wound that runs across one eye and stretches the entire length of its body.

"Good morning, sir," you say respectfully as you draw even with the rock.

The dragon stares at you coldly, and you stare back into its cloudy eye and realize that it is blind.

Flicking its tongue in and out, it continues to stare coldy at you out of its good eye, then turns away.

"I never said they'd like you," links Hinoki. "I just said you'd be safe."

With a last look at the injured dragon, you continue walking until far in the distance you see a brilliant glitter.

As you walk, the glittering increases, and soon you see that it is an immense castle, covered with gems and precious metals.

"What is this place?" you ask in awe, but Hinoki does not answer. You sigh, knowing from experience that once he is angry, nothing will make him speak until he is ready.

At long last, you reach the castle and climb a long flight of stairs more suited to the tread of dragons than men.

At the head of the stairs, you find a huge statue of a fierce-looking dragon. Its body is solid gold. Great green emeralds serve as eyes, rubies as nostrils. Layers of multicolored gems form the scales. Gossamer thin filaments of gold are woven between the outstretched wingbones. Everything is glittering and glossy except for the gaping mouth, which is strangely blackened.

At the foot of the statue, directly beneath its huge head, is a single sapphire set in the gold base. It looks like some sort of button. But what is it for? You ask Hinoki, but again there is no response.

Behind the dragon is a pair of arched doors that must surely lead into the castle. But the base of the statue blocks them completely. You stare at the statue, the button, and the doors for a long time. This must be a test. You must figure out what it is you are supposed to do. Hinoki obviously does not feel like helping you. You must figure it out yourself. After a long while you feel that you have outlined all of your choices.

1) You could push the button with your finger. Turn to page 142.

2) You might try to push the button mentally. Turn to page 126.

3) Or you could use a spell to go through the wall magically. Turn to page 108.

Hunching down in the muddy water, you back up slowly, pushing Saffron along before you.

The huge head of the hydra peers at you malevolently through the gloom, but it makes no move. Then, just as you are about to make a run for it, your foot slips on a slimy rock. Waving your arms frantically, you go down in a splash of swamp water. Instantly the great head thrusts toward you, teeth glinting in the pale light.

"Morgan!" Hinoki screams. "There are at least five other heads! One's going after Saffron! Do something—fast!"

Go back to page 60 and choose again.

"Well," you think aloud, "it does seem that man is always trying to steal your gold. So I suppose that is the right answer from your viewpoint. All right, that is my answer: love of gold."

"Wrong!" screams the dragon, blowing a cloud of black smoke over you. "Man has all the gold he needs. If man has ANY gold, it is too much!"

Horrified, you feel yourself growing smaller and smaller.

"Wait!" you scream. "That's not right! I don't agree with you!"

"Too bad!" smirks the dragon. "I told you that you couldn't win. It doesn't matter what YOU think. This is MY game!"

As the dragon's laughter echoes throughout the throne room, you realize that you and Hinoki are trapped inside the great glass globe.

"Courage, Morgan," links Hinoki as he snuggles tightly against your neck. "We'll find a way out of this somehow. Maybe it's not . . .

THE END

"Hinoki, what shall I do?" you link frantically.

"Do just what you are doing now," answers Hinoki as he presses his small silver body close to you. "Stall for time. It's our only hope! Saffron, are you with us?"

"Yes," whispers a small voice. Edging closer to the terrified girl, you clasp her small, cold hand and link, "Try to be brave. I'll do the best I can. Trust me, and above all, do what I tell you."

Turning her incredible blue eyes on you, Saffron nods her understanding.

Zed's wild laughter breaks the silent bond. Turning, you notice that the sky has grown darker. Lifting your head into the wild winds that wail around you, you see a huge shape hovering above you, blotting out the sky.

Lightning illuminates the sky, and you see the sea of lava hurling itself at the cliffs, bursting below the edge of the island and flinging molten lava at your feet.

"It comes! It comes!" Zed screams madly.

With a majesty awesome to behold, the giant black dragon flaps its wings in the storm-battered sky and slowly descends. To your wondering eyes, it seems larger than any creature you have known or even imagined. The great feet settle upon the ground in front of Zed, and the island seems to tremble. As though through a fog, you see the massive overlapping scales, each as large as your head. Vaguely you notice the missing scales and the dry, withered skin in their place. Ragged filaments stretch

between the great wing bones.

Lifting your eyes to its face, you see long, streaming tendrils, streaked with gray, trailing from its crest. The black, silver-flecked eyes, to your amazement, seem to reflect weariness.

"Who has dared to call my name, to utter the long forgotten words that have called forth the Dragon of Doom. SPEAK!" roars the dragon. Black smoke bellows from its nostrils and hides it momentarily from your view.

"It is I who called you! I, Zed, of the Council of Nine, have summoned you!"

"And what would you ask of me, O great Zed of the Council of Nine," mocks the dragon.

"I call upon you to erase man from the face of the earth forever!"

"And why should I do such a thing, Great Zed?" asks the dragon coldly.

"Why—why?" splutters Zed. "You are not to question me. You are to do as I command!"

"Do as YOU command? Who are YOU to command ME?" hisses the dragon, coiling ponderously and breathing tiny, licking flames from its nostrils.

"It is written in this book," quavers Zed, for the first time sounding uncertain as he shuffles pages rapidly.

"Do you expect ME to obey a mere book—little squiggles scrawled on a piece of paper?" roars the dragon, and a spray of acid shoots from its jaws, melting the book to nothing.

Drawing himself up to his full height, Zed throws his cloak over his shoulder haughtily and says, "I have spoken the magic words! I have summoned you, and now I command you: Go forth and destroy mankind! You may keep all the treasure you may find. It is a fair and just trade."

"And what of your companions?" murmurs the dragon, laying its great muzzle down on its clawed feet and staring at you intently all the while. "Do they command me as well?"

"This is my nephew, Morgan. My wishes are his as well," Zed says harshly, shooting you a look of warning.

"Let him speak for himself!" thunders the dragon. Then, turning its gaze back to you, it says more softly, "Come closer, young Morgan. Speak to me."

Although your legs are shaking so you feel you cannot stand, you approach the dragon bravely.

"Closer," whispers the dragon, flicking out its long red forked tongue. "My eyes are no longer the keen eyes of youth."

Wondering if each step will be your last, you walk closer and closer, halting only a few scant feet from the great claws.

"Closer still," whispers the dragon.

Climbing over the immense scaled feet, you find yourself looking directly into the dragon's black, mirrorlike eyes.

"Sit, boy. Talk to me," murmurs the dragon, its hot breath steaming about you.

"Wh-what should I talk about?" you stammer nervously.

"Tell me, boy, do you share your uncle's hatred for the world? Is it also your wish that I should destroy all mankind? Shall I start with your friend here?"

Glancing at Saffron, who stands stiff with fear at the edge of the cliff, holding Grundoon tightly in her arms, you force yourself to remain calm.

"No, O great dragon, I do not share my uncle's beliefs. I have no quarrel with the world, and I would not have called you forth."

"What would you have done with me?" whispers the dragon, a dangerous red gleam flickering in the depths of his eyes.

"I would have left you alone, as deserves a dragon of your magnificence. You have served mankind for countless ages, and now I believe you need serve no one but yourself."

"Perhaps I would enjoy destroying mankind and reaping new treasures," says the dragon.

"Then you must do so because you choose to and not because you have been ordered to do so. It must be your decision."

Behind you, Zed gives a cry of rage, but the dragon flicks its great tail threateningly, and Zed grows silent.

"You are wise for a mere manchild. Perhaps the world has become more intelligent in my absence—or did you have something to do with this, my small cousin?"

"I have tried, great one. I have been training him, since birth," says Hinoki. "But I think he has promise on his own. And the girl is rather exceptional, although she has a strange fondness for the orange monster she carries."

For a long, long moment, the dragon examines you closely. Then, like a soft wind rustling in the leaves, its mind enters yours, then slowly withdraws.

"Morgan, son of man, I wish you to return to the world and carry a message from Shen, the mighty Dragon of Doom."

"I will do your bidding, O great Shen."

"Tell them that I am no longer theirs to command. Tell them that I have vanished from their world and have taken with me the last person alive who knew the words that would summon me forth."

"Wait!" screams Zed, but the dragon wraps its long tail about him and continues.

"This is not to mean that I will no longer appear. Deeds of great evil will still waken me from my sleep, and then once more I will fly above your world, and mountains will tremble and skies will weep. Whenever destruction and death walk the land, you will know that I am abroad, and you will be warned. Then you must seek to repair the wrongs that have been wrought or incur my wrath!"

"Why are you doing this? You are the Dragon of Doom!" protests Zed.

"I am old. I have seen much death and destruction. I have all the treasure a dragon could ever need. All I wish is to sleep and be warm and dream of past glories. But if the evil of the world should ever outweigh its goodness, I shall appear and restore the balance. That is my message. Will you remember it?"

"Yes, sir," you answer faintly.

"Good. Take this with you." And reaching up, the dragon plucks one of its long, silvery tendrils out of its crest and hands it to you.

Smooth and warm, it glistens like a polished metal ribbon in your hands.

"It will protect you against all dragons and will shelter our small cousin against her furry fanged creature."

"What about me?" screeches Zed.

"Farewell," says the dragon, ignoring the plea. And rising to its feet, it shakes its great wings and slithers to one end of the island, Zed still clutched tightly in its tail.

You and Saffron cling to each other as the great winds rise. At last the great wings fill the air, and the dragon soars into the reddened sky. You watch until the Dragon of Doom and Zed are only a small dot in the sky and then finally fade from sight.

THE END

"I'm sorry, but that's not possible. My pseudo-dragon, Hinoki, never leaves my side. Besides, you wouldn't want him to. He'd eat every animal in the place."

"That's not true!" squawks Hinoki silently.

"Do you want to sleep in a barn?" you link.

"Well, carry on, Morgan, but be careful. I sense mischief in this fellow."

"Please show me to my room. It's been a long day," you say.

"Won't you have more cider, sir, to ease your slumbers?" the innkeeper asks oilily.

"No more," hisses Hinoki.

Normally you like cider, but this brew has an odd flavor. "Thanks, but I don't think I'll have any trouble sleeping. I'm very tired."

"Follow me, please," says the innkeeper as he leads you down a dark corridor.

"Aren't there any lights?" you ask as you feel your way down the dark corridor.

"I try to save a few coins, here and there, by saving candles, but no matter, here's your room, just through this door. I'll bid you good night now and see you on the morrow."

Your outstretched hands touch the outline of a door, and you grope for the doorknob. Silently it swings open before your hand.

"Danger!" screams Hinoki. Instantly you drop to the floor, expecting an attack of some sort, but nothing happens.

"What's—what's the matter?" you question nervously.

"Something's wrong. Don't you feel that cold,

damp breeze and smell that air? It smells more like a dungeon than a bedroom."

Cautiously you reach out, and your hand touches—nothing! As you explore more, you feel stone walls covered with slime.

Suddenly you hear footsteps. You roll onto your back, reach out in a wide sweep, and grab what feels like a leg. Swiftly you jerk the leg, heaving the body toward the doorway.

"Try to murder me, will you?" you snarl.

You hear a thin whimper, and you realize that you are not holding the innkeeper but someone else. Instinctively your hand tightens around the leg, and although there is a sickening thump as the body strikes the slimy wall of the floorless room, you do not release your grip. Slowly you edge your way back from the yawning edge, dragging the unknown person with you. At last both of you are firmly wedged against a far wall.

"Who are you?" you ask roughly as you shake the small figure in your grasp. "Speak up. I could have killed you just now. If I don't get the right answers, I may do so yet."

"Sounds good to me," links Hinoki.

"It's me, Saffron," says a meek voice you recognize as the girl in the dining hall. "I—I was checking to see if you were still alive and if I could help you."

As you clutch the small, thin figure, it seems that you can feel her heart pounding through her tattered clothing.

"You knew he would try to kill me?"

"Of course. That's why I tried to warn you, but you wouldn't listen."

Unbidden, the picture of the girl shaking her head from side to side leaps into your mind.

"Why should he try to kill me?"

"A man—a strange man—passed through yesterday. He frightened the customers away. After they left, he told my master that if anyone followed him or asked about him, my master was to prevent him from following. And if my master failed, the stranger would come back and kill him. My master did not believe him and tried to throw him out, but when he touched him, his hands blistered as though he had scalded them in fire. After that, my master was frightened and argued no more. He isn't a bad man, but he is a coward."

"And aren't you afraid?"

"Yes, but I couldn't let him kill you," whispers the girl.

"We should leave before the innkeeper comes back!" Hinoki mind-links.

"I agree," says Saffron. "We can go to my room. He'd never believe I'd defy him."

"You can hear our thoughts?" you ask, surprised.

"I can hear everyone's thoughts," answers Saffron, "not just yours."

"But—"

"Not now, Morgan," urges Hinoki. "Let's get to safety. Then we can talk."

Holding Saffron's arm and tracing the wall with your hand, you proceed down the corridor to her tiny room next to the kitchen.

As Saffron strikes flint to candle, you hear a hiss and see the glint of sharp white fangs, and suddenly an orange body flashes through the air. Instantly the air is filled with shrill hissing and screeching sounds. Hinoki's sharp claws puncture your leather shoulder pad and cut into your flesh. Then your face is raked by a spread of cold, white pain.

"Grundoon! Stop that! Bad boy!" scolds Saffron as she pulls an enormous orange tomcat, spitting and clawing, from you.

"Bad boy!" you exclaim as you try to calm your wildly flapping pseudo-dragon.

"Grundoon didn't mean anything by that. We frightened him. Please don't be angry with him. He's my only friend," pleads Saffron.

Glaring at the huge cat, who glares back with malice, you tuck Hinoki under your arm protectively and settle onto the hard bed.

"Settle down, Grundoon. You will not eat him—not now, not ever!" Saffron links.

You sit up, startled—you know that others can mind-link with pseudo-dragons, but you have never heard of anyone mind-linking with a cat! And how is it that you are able to hear her thoughts?

Please turn the page.

"It's quite simple," Saffron says, noticing your puzzlement. "I'm not a witch or anything. It's this medallion." She removes a small medal, shaped like a cat with wings, from around her neck. "My father was a traveling tinker. He bought, sold, traded, and sometimes stole. He gave me this so I could help him with his schemes—like stealing horses and livestock."

"Where is he now?" you ask.

"Dead. He was caught with six cows that weren't his, and they hanged him. I was given to the innkeeper to raise in exchange for work."

"Why do you stay?" asks Hinoki.

"Because I have nowhere else to go."

You look at the tiny medallion hanging at the end of the thin chain. "Saffron, will you sell me your medallion? Hinoki and I are on a dangerous mission, and your medallion just might make the different between life and death."

"Oh, I couldn't!" gasps Saffron as her hand closes protectively around the medallion. "It's all I have left of my father."

"Saffron, why don't you come with us?" links Hinoki. Seeing your startled reaction, the excited pseudo-dragon goes on. "Hush, Morgan. Let me finish. Saffron, this mission could well affect all mankind. If you don't help us, life might even be worse for you than it is now. Please say you'll come."

"I wouldn't go anywhere without Grundoon," says Saffron.

"That man-eater?" you whisper. "Never!"

The three of you continue your discussion for hours. Grundoon sits on Saffron's lap, purring gently through his fangs and eyeing you with suspicion from time to time. At last you give in. Saffron—and Grundoon—will join you.

Dawn sees you many miles from the inn, following Zed's trail.

"What do we do now?" you ask as you stare bleakly at the road that divides at your feet. "Which way did he go?"

You sit down at the base of a tree and link minds with Hinoki, but although you strain your abilities to the utmost, you are unable to find your uncle on either path.

"You try, Saffron," you urge, ignoring Grundoon, who frolics happily on the grass. Holding her medallion to her forehead, Saffron closes her eyes and concentrates.

"Nothing," she says at last. "I get nothing."

"Well, then we must make a good guess,"

says Hinoki. "Where do these roads lead, Saffron?"

"The one on the left goes into the Forlorn Mountains. The road on the right goes into the Great Swamp. Both are filled with danger and many roaming monsters. All we can do is pick one."

1) If you want to take the trail toward the Forlorn Mountains, turn to page 112.

2) If you want to enter the Great Swamp, turn to page 133.

You open the door marked "THIS WAY IN" and see a tunnel loom above you, outlined by a soft glow. Flapping your wings hesitantly, you rise and settle softly in the mouth of the tunnel. You see nothing that looks even remotely dangerous. The only unusual thing about it is a slight current of air that flows around you, ruffling your wings and whispering across your face.

"Hinoki, why don't we check out this tunnel? It seems safe enough."

"I don't know, Morgan. There's something odd about this. It looks wrong somehow. I don't know what, but something about it bothers me."

"Well, it's better than the other choices, and there's a nice cool breeze blowing through it. That must mean that it's leading somewhere. I think we should go this way." Without waiting for an answer, you plunge into the tunnel.

"All right, Morgan. I'm with you," links Hinoki. "I just hope we don't regret this."

At first all goes well. Then the tunnel begins to curve gently, and the flow of air grows stronger. As you follow the curves, you realize it can no longer be called a breeze. It's definitely a wind, and you find it difficult to retain your balance.

"Morgan, I'm having trouble staying aloft," gasps Hinoki. And as you glance at him, he flips over backward, seemingly out of control.

"I'm coming, Hinoki!" you link, but as you labor with your wing muscles, nothing happens, and you drift off to your right until you too are caught by the wind and blown head over heels after Hinoki.

"Help! Hinoki! I can't do anything, either. The wind has got me!"

Harder and harder blows the wind. Faster and faster the two of you tumble before it. Then the wind seems to rise straight up, whirling around and around, faster and faster like a tornado, carrying the two of you with it.

Suddenly you slam into something hard that forces all the air out of you. You strain to see what you have crashed into, but although you can feel it, you see nothing.

The wind continues to push against you with greater and greater force, and then, at last, there is a terrible stretching noise, and with a loud POP! you and Hinoki are thrust out of the tunnel.

Please turn to page 148.

"I'm going to use Zed's ring of wishes," you say as you open the thong that binds the small bag given you by the council.

"No, Morgan. It's too dangerous. It's too powerful for you to use, and we don't know what will happen. It could kill you," argues Hinoki.

"Those hydra heads aren't exactly thinking of my health," you say as you place the ring on your finger. It slides on loosely, yet even as you look at it, wondering how to use it, it begins to shrink until it fits your finger perfectly. Touching the ring with the fingers of your right hand, you point the ring at the hydra and shout, "I wish you would disappear forever!"

One moment you are looking straight into the cold, staring eyes of the fearsome monster. The next instant, the hydra is gone—completely vanished!

"Where did it go, Morgan?" whispers Saffron, peering out from behind you.

"I don't know and I don't care, as long as it stays gone."

"Thank goodness the ring worked and nothing terrible happened to any of us," says Hinoki. "One can never be sure with such a powerful item. However, you should think about one thing. Some rings of this sort are only good for three wishes. You just used one of them. We don't know if there are any wishes left. If we should get in trouble in the future, we won't be able to count on the ring."

"The future is still the future," you say as you take the ring off and place it back in the little sack. "I'm just glad we're alive and still have a future to consider. Come on, let's get going before that hydra's big brother comes looking for it."

Please turn to page 32.

Reluctantly you move toward a small gold cask overflowing with pearls and diamonds at one side of the chamber.

You move very carefully, sliding first one foot, then another, ready to leap back should a trap appear.

As you slide farther and farther, it seems to you that you are walking at a slight downward angle. You look behind you, and indeed it does seem as though the floor is slanted slightly. You feel a flutter of worry and decide to go back, but it doesn't seem possible. Somehow the slant seems to increase the more you struggle, and the more you struggle, the more you slip backward.

You fling yourself down on the floor and scramble desperately, trying to pull yourself back. But it doesn't work.

There is a low grumble, like a machine grinding into gear, and then the entire floor turns on its side and dumps you into total darkness.

Flailing helplessly with your arms, you fall for what seems like an eternity.

You realize you must do something immediately if you are to remain alive.

1) If you decide to use a fly spell, turn to page 26.

2) If you decide to use the wish ring to grow wings, turn to page 45.

"How far away is the barn you mentioned?" you ask.

"It's on the other side of the hill, a half mile away," says the innkeeper.

"That's too far, Morgan," argues Hinoki. "We can't link if we're that far apart."

You try to think, but it feels as if there is sand in your head. You do not reply.

You hear Hinoki's voice as you sprawl sleepily on the table. Weakly you try to respond, but soon you are sound asleep.

Hinoki regards you with disgust, then hops over to the shoulder of the silent girl, and the pair of them leave the room.

Sometime later, you feel the innkeeper shaking you. You stagger to your feet, leaning on him.

You wonder vaguely what's the matter with your feet. You also wonder why you are having so much trouble going down the ladder into the dark, dank dirt cellar. CELLAR?

You open your mouth to ask the innkeeper why you are in a cellar, but your voice doesn't seem to work, and your outstretched hands find nothing but cold stone walls.

The darkness presses in on all sides as you collapse. As your aching head sinks to your chest, you realize that you have been drugged.

Maybe Hinoki was right. Maybe your uncle set a trap for you to prevent you from stopping him!

Struggling weakly, you try to link with Hinoki, but nothing happens.

"Maybe in the morning . . ." you think as you drift off to sleep. "Maybe in the morning . . ."

THE END

Once more you take to the air, but now things are different. You are well fed, and even better, you have a plan.

On and on you fly through dark and twisting corridors. You round a final bend and enter the most incredible room you have ever seen. Cut from clear black stone, the walls rise in smooth arches to a high vaulted ceiling. The top of the room is so high you can barely see it. The black rock sparkles and gleams as though it contains an inner life.

The floor of the room is buried in treasure, which lies heaped to the farthest stretches of the room. In the center of the room, rising out of a small mountain of gold and gems, is an immense black throne.

"Whose—whose throne is that?" you whisper in awe.

"Why, the Great Dragon's, of course," answers Pearl. "He should be here. He always knows when someone comes."

Suddenly the air begins to vibrate with a strange humming sound. Looking up, you see a huge figure descending. The air whistles about you, and you clutch Hinoki tightly and move closer to Pearl's comforting bulk.

The Great Dragon coils itself upon its throne, and Pearl hurries forward. "O Great Dragon," she exclaims, "I'm so happy to see you. What is happening in Dragon Land? This manchild has been telling me horrible stories. What can we do? We must protect ourselves from this Zed!"

Pearl gestures at you, and you look straight

into the steely eyes of the Great Dragon.

"Come forth, manchild, and let me look at you closer," it says in a deep voice.

Quivering with fear, you step forward.

"Tell me the stories you have told Pearl," the Great Dragon booms.

You tell the Great Dragon about the council and your mission and your travels and all that has happened to you.

"Yes," muses the Great Dragon. "I knew that something was wrong, but I wasn't sure what. Now I know."

"But now it is too late!" cackles an evil voice, and out of the shadows steps your Uncle Zed. "It is too late for you and all your kind!" sneers Zed. "I'm going to spare you the trouble of dying slowly. I'll kill all of you off at one time!"

Silver eyes sparking with rage, the Great Dragon rears up and looses a massive jet of hot steam. Zed raises one little finger, and the steam bounces back harmlessly.

The Great Dragon hisses angrily and looses a great gush of flame. Again the flame strikes the invisible barrier and bounces back.

"You can't hurt me!" cackles Zed. "I am too powerful. There is only one who could kill me, and even he must do my bidding!"

Suddenly the air crackles around you, and lightning erupts somewhere above you. Looking up, you see another dragon, much larger than the Great Dragon, plummeting toward you.

"Behold your doom!" screams Zed over the fierce winds that whip through the room.

"Great Shen, Dragon of Doom, I command you to kill all who are present! They are my enemies!"

Instantly the silver dragon rises to meet Shen, and they collide in midair.

Fang, flame, and claw struggle for supremacy in the air above you. You hold your breath in fear and hold Hinoki so tightly that he squeaks. One minute it seems that surely the black dragon will win, and the next it seems the silver dragon must triumph.

Blood pours from the wounded dragons and burns holes wherever it lands. Zed dances and laughs loudly. Pearl weeps great dragon tears and buries her head under her wing.

"We must do something, Hinoki!" you exclaim.

"Let's try linking with them, Morgan. I doubt they'll ever hear us or that it will do any good, but at least we can try."

Zed laughs hysterically as the two of you place your heads together, concentrating with all your might, and project your thoughts toward the great dragons battling above you.

"Stop fighting!" you link, hoping your message is reaching the dragons. "You are not enemies. Why are you fighting? Because some insignificant human tells you to do so?"

There is a short pause in the battle. Concentrating harder, you continue projecting thoughts of peace.

Then, as you are beginning to despair, the silver dragon slips from the black dragon's grasp and circles down to his throne.

Flanks heaving, blood streaming from his body, the silver dragon gasps, "You are right. I have no quarrel with the mighty Shen. Come down, brother. Let us talk."

"No!" screams Zed. "Kill him!"

The Dragon of Doom circles slowly, and you see the dreadful wounds it has suffered. You also notice for the first time how ancient it is. Its teeth are blunted with age, and its claws are bent and broken and many scales are missing.

The Dragon of Doom descends slowly and lands staring at you intently.

"What you say has merit, manchild. I assume my small cousin has taught you your wisdom. What would you have us do?"

"Kill him! Don't listen to him!" screams Zed. "I have commanded you! You must do my bidding!"

"I obey no man!" rumbles the black dragon. "True, you have uttered the words to summon me forth, but dragons are not the puppets of men. I, Shen, the Dragon of Doom, decide my own destiny!"

"But—" Zed begins, but the Dragon of Doom flicks out its tail and encircles Zed in its coils, then roars, "Silence!"

"Speak, manchild," says the black dragon. And quickly you tell your story. From time to time, Zed tries to interrupt, but each time the black dragon tightens its coiled tail, and Zed is silenced.

When you are finished, the two great dragons

eye you closely, and you think you see a look of approval in their eyes.

"I was afraid that goodness, innocence, bravery, and love had all but disappeared from the world," says the black dragon. "I was ready to do as this man has bid me, but I see now that I was wrong." Turning to the silver dragon, the Dragon of Doom says, "I apologize for any injuries I may have caused. My actions were misguided. Please forgive me."

"This will be a story to tell my grandchildren," replies the silver dragon, smiling. "But what shall we do with this evil man?" The Great Dragon gestures toward Zed.

Lifting Zed high, Shen stares straight into his eyes angrily. "I could kill him, since he is so anxious to bring death upon others."

"That would be too easy," answers the silver dragon. "I have another plan that might be more suitable." And he gestures toward a large black glass globe that sits beside his throne. Black mists swirl inside its depths, and occasionally you notice something flitting at the glass, like a fish in a bowl.

"I have found this globe useful for holding those who are foolish enough to try to steal my treasure," says the silver dragon. "It amuses me to keep the thieves there."

"Excellent!" booms the great black dragon as he hands Zed to the silver dragon. And then, before your astonished eyes, Zed shrinks to the size of your smallest fingernail and disappears!

Both dragons peer into the globe, and for the

barest instant, you see your uncle, his mouth open in a silent scream of rage, floating inside the globe. Then the black mists close about him and he is gone.

"And now for you," breathes the great Dragon of Doom. You recoil in terror, until you realize the dragon is handing you one of its scales that was lost in battle. Glossy black and nearly as large as you are, the huge scale radiates a feeling of power.

"Take this scale. Use it as a shield. It will keep you from harm. It expresses my pleasure that mankind is indeed worth saving."

"And I offer you this token of my appreciation," says the silver dragon, handing you a curved silver claw, also lost in the battle. "Seat it in a hilt of silver, and you will have the finest dagger in the land. It will turn any blow and warn you when enemies are present. And now, my cousin and I have much to discuss. Pearl will return you to your own land. Take our blessings with you."

As Pearl rises into the air, you and Hinoki wave until the black Dragon of Doom and the silver Great Dragon grow smaller and smaller, then finally disappear.

THE END

"Why didn't I study my spells harder," you mutter, but after thinking hard for several minutes, you remember the words to the pass wall spell. Crossing your fingers for luck, you utter them.

Instantly strange things begin to happen. There is a sick feeling in the pit of your stomach, and your body seems to break up into a million tiny dots and drift toward the wall. You cringe as you near the massive stones, but your body floats forward and then passes into the rock itself. You feel as though you are swimming through mud, and you almost panic when you try to draw a breath.

Forcing yourself to remain calm, you move slowly forward. At last one hand breaks free, and you are clear of the wall, standing on solid ground inside the castle. You draw a deep breath as the millions of dots reform and you become whole once more.

"You did that very well, Morgan. I'm proud of you," says Hinoki as he reforms and reappears on your shoulder. "You were sleeping in class that day, as I recall. I didn't think you'd remember the words."

Hot words bubble to your lips, but you bite them back, remembering that what he says is true. You were asleep. But fortunately the words stuck in your memory anyhow.

Please turn to page 21.

Rolling and crawling awkwardly, you stumble to the campfire, pulling the vines with you. Flinging yourself backward, you land with the shambler under you, in the fire. A terrible smell of scorched rottenness fills your nose, and the mound presses itself against your body. More vines begin to wrap themselves around you till you can hardly breathe.

"Help! Do something! This isn't working!" you call desperately.

Go back to page 55 and choose again.

Struggling against the terrible force of the air current, you unfurl your wings. Instantly they are plastered against each other. You grunt and strain, pressing against the wind, but it is useless.

As you spin about, trying to open your wings, you push yourself out of the main stream of air and into a slower air current up against the side of the tunnel.

Spreading your arms and legs against the rough rock surface, you hang on for dear life! As Hinoki plunges by, you reach out and pluck him from the air. Even his slight weight is enough to pull you off balance, and for a sickening moment, you teeter back and forth over the black abyss. Then your prayers are answered as you catch your balance, and the two of you cling precariously to the wall.

"I thought we were gone for sure," links Hinoki nervously.

Please turn to page 56.

As the three of you trudge up into the unfriendly mountains, you wonder if you will find your uncle soon. Surely he cannot be as terrible as Hinoki and Saffron think. Surely it must all be a mistake.

"No mistake," says Saffron. "He kept smiling secretly to himself, and there was something about a dragon."

By early afternoon, you have climbed to the top of a tall peak. You are surrounded on all sides by a bleak, desolate landscape. Gray emptiness stretches away in all directions. Nowhere can you find a sign that Zed has been there. Hinoki takes to the air, his wings outstretched to catch the sweeping air currents. You link minds, but nothing stirs beneath your shared gaze other than birds and small animals. Using her medallion, Saffron also casts her mind in all directions, listening, hoping to hear some hint of even the smallest thought.

"I'm sorry," she says. "There's an orc sleeping in a cave not far away, and he's having some rather bloody dreams, but that's all I can find."

You have obviously chosen the wrong path. You must retrace your steps and head out into the Great Swamp.

Please turn to page 133.

"I don't like either of your choices. Love is my answer," you say.

"That is not one of the choices!" roars the dragon. "I do not accept your answer!"

"Well, I do not accept your choices!" you say fiercely. "And it is true. Think about a mother's love for her child. Think about all the acts of courage and bravery that have been done by humans in the name of love."

"I know of no such acts," the dragon says coldly. "Would you care to put your belief to the test? If you win, I will help you with your mission. If you lose, you die!"

"Of course. I know what I say is right. I will agree to your test. What do I do?"

"I will imprison one of you in my glass globe. The imprisonment will be brief . . . forever! You must decide which of you it is to be."

Stunned, your mind reels in shock. If you choose Hinoki's freedom, perhaps the dragon will keep his word and aid you. But if he doesn't, you could be trapped in the globe forever.

"Hinoki, what should I do?" you link.

"You must do what you think best, Morgan. I know you will choose correctly," answers Hinoki.

1) If you choose to have Hinoki put in the globe and save yourself, turn to page 117.

2) If you choose to save Hinoki and have yourself put in the globe, turn to page 153.

"We'll help," you say. "Saffron, give me your hands. This is what we'll do. . . ."

Minutes later, you are ready. You sit in the mud next to Saffron, with the couatl lying across both your laps. Its once-silver scales are now a dull gray. Its eyes are closed, and its breathing seems ragged.

Somewhat nervously, Hinoki steps off your shoulder and stands on the couatl's back. You and Saffron form a circle around Hinoki, with your hands resting on the couatl. Then you place your foreheads against Hinoki's head.

"Saffron, think of blue skies and soft, floating clouds. It's very warm, and you feel very good," you say softly. "You are filled with thoughts of power. You can do anything you set your mind to. Now our friend, the couatl's, scales are growing warm beneath our touch, beneath our love. Our thoughts are going into its body and carrying our love. The couatl is healing now. Our caring is flowing through its body, healing all the pains."

You concentrate as you have never concentrated before. You feel your mind flow through the couatl's body. You are used to Hinoki's mind blending with yours, but the added presence of Saffron gives you power that you have never had before. Just to make sure of success, you return mentally to the couatl's head and think your way through its body a second time, willing it to become healthy.

As you open your eyes, the couatl stirs. Looking down, you see that its scales now shine

brightly, and its feathers are like a shimmering rainbow. Its eyes sparkle with health, and as its tongue flicks in and out, it almost seems to smile.

"You have restored my strength. I am forever in your debt. Tell me what I can do for you, and if I have the power, it is yours."

"We are searching for the same man who attacked you," you say. "He is my uncle."

The couatl scans you intently. "You are very different from your uncle," it says at last.

"I have never met him," you admit.

"But once, he was a great and good magic-user. We are trying to find him and bring him back to the Council of Nine."

"There is no good left in him," says the couatl. "I can tell you his destination, however. He is going to World's End. It is there that he plans his revenge upon the world."

"World's End?" you say. "What's that?"

"It is thought to be the end of the world," answers the couatl, "a strange place indeed. I do not venture there often. It is full of volcanoes and swirling mist. The sun never shines, and monsters roam freely. It is not a place for lawful folks to be."

"Still, that is where we must go."

"I will seek help," says the couatl. "I do not think you should go there. But if you must, I will bring help and follow as soon as possible."

Please turn to page 53.

"I have been charged by the Council of Nine to complete my mission, and I must do so. But I love Hinoki, and I will not let you do this to him." And without a clear idea of what you will do, you rush toward the Great Dragon.

You actually get as far as the throne before a cloud of black smoke surrounds you, and you feel yourself shrinking, shrinking, shrinking. Then you are picked up and placed inside the black globe.

You peer out at the Great Dragon, who holds Hinoki balanced on a single silver claw, and hear it say, "You know, he almost had me convinced, in spite of myself."

You beat upon the glass in despair.

"Don't worry, Morgan," links Hinoki. "I'll get you out somehow!" And as the black smoke obscures the dragons from view, you hope with all your heart that this is not . . .

TIIE END

Curiously, you look around you. The island is larger than it appeared at first. Made entirely of the glassy black stone, it seems to harbor no life of any sort.

"Where is Zed?" asks Saffron. "I thought he'd be up here."

"I don't know, but the island's bigger than it looks. Maybe there's something we can't see. Hinoki, you take the right side of the island. Saffron and I will take the left side. Holler if you see anything. Saffron, you try for an ESP detect, just in case he's hidden."

"Morgan, I'm going to let the cat out of the bag, if you don't mind. He's going crazy in there, and he can't hurt anything up here."

"All right," you say reluctantly as Saffron opens the bag and shakes out a very angry Grundoon. To your surprise, instead of attacking you or doing something equally dreadful, the cat sits at Saffron's feet and starts to groom itself as though nothing had happened.

"Come on, Saffron. Let's get going. Use your amulet as we walk and see if you can pick up any stray thoughts."

The two of you walk around the edges of the black glass island without seeing anything. The edges fall straight into the ocean of lava, which crashes against the sheer walls below. Above, there is nothing but the empty sky filled with heavy clouds reflecting the angry red sea below.

"Morgan, I can't find anything with the amulet. I don't think there's anyone but us up here. And the walls are so steep, I don't see how anyone could be hiding down there. Grundoon, why are you acting like that? Stop it, you silly cat!"

Grundoon is crouched at your feet, his back arched like a drawn bow, with every hair on his body standing stiffly upright. Taking tiny, mincing steps, he growls deep in his throat and hisses menacingly.

"What's your crazy cat up to now?" you sigh as Grundoon presses himself firmly against your leg.

"I don't know," says Saffron. "He usually only does that when he's scared of something. But I haven't seen anything to be afraid of."

"What a fool I've been!" you cry, clapping a hand to your head. "Saffron, just because we don't see something doesn't mean it's not here. Zed is a high-level magic-user. He could hide himself with any number of spells, and we'd never be able to detect him."

"You mean he could be two feet away from us and we wouldn't even know it?" whispers Saffron.

"Sure—but you don't have to whisper. I'm sure he's not that close. Oh, Grundoon, quit crowding me!" you say impatiently, giving the cat a shove with your leg. Without really meaning to, you use too much strength. Grundoon flies through the air and then slams into something in midflight. Yowling horribly, he stretches his long, sharp claws and tries to save himself from falling.

A muffled curse comes from nowhere. Then, before your startled eyes, a hand clutches Grundoon's neck—a hand that is soon joined by the rest of a body.

You stare silently at the small wrinkled figure standing before you, glowering with hatred.

"Uncle Zed?"

"I am no one's uncle," sneers the old man. "You are nothing to me!"

"But you mean something to me," you say respectfully. And quickly you tell your uncle of your mission. "Long have I thought of you," you add. "You were my guiding light when I was a small boy. I never tired of hearing the stories of your marvelous deeds. I yearn to be as great a magic-user as you when I grow up."

"What use have I for goodness and light? Only weaklings have need for them. All that is powerful—all that is important in life—is evil. I have pledged my life to serving evil, and now I will reap its rewards.

"If you are truly my nephew, I offer you the chance to join me. We alone will live, while the rest of the world dies. If you are not with me, you are against me, and you can die along with the rest. What say you?"

You look around, dazed. Saffron stands frozen, clasping Grundoon to her chest. Her red hair blows wildly about her frightened face, her eyes blue and clear in the strange light reflected from the sky.

"What about Saffron?" you cry over the rising wind.

"The girl doesn't matter. No one matters. She will die along with the rest. You must decide

quickly. Give me your answer. The hour is at hand! The Dragon of Doom approaches!"

The sky is filled with jagged flashes of lightning, and the clouds churn madly, glowing orange and yellow and green. Below the cliffs, you hear the crash of the lava cascading against the black walls. The wind whistles past your ears, keening a song of madness.

"DECIDE!" screams your uncle.

1) "I will do it!" you cry. "I will cast my fate with yours!" If this is your decision, turn to page 52.

2) "I cannot do as you ask, nor can I believe that anyone can hate the world so much. It's not too late to change your mind and return with me." If this is what you choose to tell your uncle, turn to page 131.

3) "I would like to do as you ask," you say, stalling desperately for time, "but I'm confused. May I consult my pseudo-dragon?" If this is your choice, turn to page 79.

"Innkeeper, I will stay here tonight, and that's final! Now please bring me something to eat and drink."

The innkeeper's face twitches, but he bows low and vanishes into the kitchen. As you settle yourself in front of the hearth, you notice the girl staring at you with her big blue eyes.

You study the room to hide the fact that her gaze is making you very uncomfortable. Quick glances tell you that she is still standing in the doorway. Her incredible blue eyes fill with tears and shine with disappointment.

You are extremely uncomfortable. The girl is making you wonder whether or not you were right. You don't even know her, but somehow it matters.

1) If you want to change your mind and leave now, turn to page 68.

2) If you refuse to change your mind and want to ignore the girl, turn to page 28.

Closing your eyes tightly to the horror that enfolds you, you picture the words of the spell in your old textbook. Concentrating on the words, you speak them aloud. Instantly you feel Hinoki's familiar mental nudge and Saffron's soft touch as their minds lend you strength. The spell bursts from your mind and seems to explode around you. Slowly the vines unwind, and you roll free and fall upon the ground, gasping for breath.

"Go away, mound, and never come back!" you whisper hoarsely. Without a sound, the heap of rotting vegetation lumbers into the swamp and disappears.

"Are you all right, Morgan?" asks Hinoki as he perches on your chest and peers into your face. "I—I was quite concerned."

"No more than I was, I'm sure, old friend," you say as you sit up slowly.

A close check of your campsite discloses nothing else of danger, and your small party finally settles back to spend a quiet night in the swamp.

Please turn to page 58.

"You're sure you won't forget what to do?" Hinoki links nervously.

"I'm sure. Don't worry," you answer as you take out the bag of holding. But you are anything but sure.

Swiftly the wind walker storms toward you, sucking air into its great cheeks. Just as swiftly, you retreat to a far corner of the huge hall.

Placing your thumbs into the neck of the bag, you wait tensely as the wind walker fills its cheeks till they will hold no more, then blows its great blast of icy air at you. You bend your knees, utter the magic words of the jump spell, and leap straight up into the air.

You have timed your leap carefully, and the icy blast of air hides your escape. As you start to descend, you open the bag of holding to its fullest. Hinoki, clinging to your shoulders, tries desperately to guide your descent.

So far, the wind walker has not been able to locate you. It kneels where you last stood and pokes through the piled treasure. At the last moment, it raises its head. Clouds of confusion cross its face as it spots you, and quickly it starts to fill its cheeks once more. But it is too late.

Screaming loudly, you crash down, pulling the bag of holding over the startled creature. The bag expands magically, and scrambling to keep your balance, you tie the bag up triumphantly and jump for joy. "We did it, Hinoki!"

"Indeed we did, Morgan. Indeed we did."

Please turn to page 61.

Concentrating fiercely, you start at your toes and slowly force all your energy upward. Then you draw it together mentally and, focusing on the button, unleash it in a great stream of pure energy.

The invisible beam crackles as it strikes the button. Then, just as you suspected, a great burst of flame shoots from the statue's mouth and blackens the spot where you stood moments before.

You feel very pleased with yourself as the doors to the castle swing open, and a figure with a fanged snout appears on the top step and glares down at you.

"I suppose you think that you should get in, just because you figured out the trap," it snarls.

"I—I really had hoped we could come in," you stammer. "Is that possible?"

"Is that possible?" mimics the lizard man doorkeeper. "No, it's not possible. Can't you read?" And stepping aside, he points to a small sign tacked to the foot of the door that reads "NO PEOPLE ALLOWED."

"Your kind isn't welcome here," snarls the lizard man, his yellow eyes blinking evilly. "Go away." Before you can speak, he steps into the castle and starts to close the door.

"Don't!" booms a small but commanding voice, and the lizard man freezes in place. With a shock, you realize it was Hinoki who spoke.

"It is I who wishes to enter the castle," continues Hinoki. "Pay no attention to this human.

Stand aside and let me enter or I shall be angry."

"Excuse me, sir. I did not notice you at first," snivels the doorkeeper. "I am only a lowly lizard man. Of course you may enter, but the human will have to remain outside. Perhaps you could tie it to a tree."

"You begin to annoy me," says Hinoki. "Take me to your superior."

"But, sir," wails the lizard man, "they'll have my scales if I let another human in. An old man named Zed forced me to let him in two days ago, and he's caused terrible trouble. If they don't catch him, the dragons will banish me to the desert!"

"Zed's been this way!" you exclaim. "You've got to let us in! I can help you. My mission is to bring him back to the Council of Nine."

"Is this the truth?" asks the lizard man, his yellow eyes glowing with excitement. "Can you really get rid of him for me?"

"It is our mission—which, may I remind you, we cannot accomplish as long as you keep us standing out here," Hinoki says loftily.

"Please enter," says the lizard man as he stands aside and gestures you in. "But remember," he growls as you pass, "if you fail and I get sent to the desert, I may just eat my mistakes!"

"Don't worry," you say with more confidence than you feel. "We won't fail."

Please turn to page 21.

The shambling mound draws you closer and closer, wrapping you ever more firmly in its vines! You are finding it hard to breathe, and the air smells like rotting vegetables. Now the slime is soaking through your clothes and coating your body with foul stickiness.

"Hold still! I'm going to stab it," cries Saffron as she plunges her blade downward. "It doesn't seem to do any good. It doesn't even seem to be bothered!"

"Do something quick!" you gasp as a creeper encircles your neck and begins to squeeze.

"Morgan! It's got my knife!" screams Saffron.

Go back to page 55 and choose again.

As you open the door, you are forced forward and down, and a great wave of wind sucks you through the doorway into blackness.

You try to cling frantically to the rocks on the side of the tunnel, but to no avail. You are rolled around like a tidbit on a giant's plate before the wind finally slurps you down. And down. And down.

"Another fine mess you've gotten us into!" grumbles Hinoki as the two of you tumble over and over and you fall faster and faster past jagged rock outcroppings.

"No, wait! I forgot! I have wings! You have wings, too! We can just put out our wings and we'll stop!"

"Don't try it!" Hinoki links sharply. "We're too close to the walls, and we're falling too fast. If we put out our wings, they'd be ripped off!"

1) "But we have to do something!" you scream. If we're going to die anyhow, it doesn't matter! Let's try to fly!" Turn to page 111.

2) "Grab on to one of these rocks!" yells Hinoki. "We'll climb down till we find a way out." Turn to page 56.

Zed's mouth opens, and a terrible dry sound issues from his thin lips. With a start, you realize that he is laughing!

"Fool!" hisses Zed, all signs of humor absent from his sharp features. "What have you to offer that could compare to what I shall gain from the Dragon of Doom?"

"I offer you love, understanding, and the respect of your peers."

"Ha! What do I care about such matters? I dismissed them long ago, early on in my years of exile. Where were all those who cared about me then when I needed them?"

"Uncle, there have always been those who care about you. My mother, your sister, died with your name on her lips. You were never forgotten."

"I no longer care for your world or anything in it. But those few who are left alive after the dragon comes will have cause to remember me. My name shall be legend!"

"Your name will be hated! You will be cursed by the entire world!" you scream above the rising wind that whips your words away.

Ignoring you, your uncle lifts his hands toward the lightning-lashed sky and laughs maniacally at the sight of an enormous shape that fills the sky above you.

Doom is almost upon you. If you want one last chance to survive, return to page 122 and choose again.

Standing firmly on the floor, you place the gold ring on your finger and point toward all the corners. Even as you watch, the ring, which is several sizes too large, shrinks to fit your finger.

"O magic wish ring," you say nervously, "please tell me if there are any traps in this chamber."

"Simultaneously a mysterious voice intones, "Yesss!" as Hinoki links, "No! You have to be very specific," he groans. "You have wasted a wish."

"I'm sorry," you mumble. "What should we do now?"

"I don't know," sighs Hinoki. "All we know for sure is that there's a trap here somewhere. I suppose we could risk using the ring again, but we should probably save it for another time when we really need it. Some of these rings have only three wishes in them, and some have more. And maybe your uncle used some of them before we got it."

"I don't think we should use it again. He'll probably be angry that we even used it. It's his, after all."

"Well, then, I suppose we'd better try something else," links Hinoki.

Go back to page 21 and choose again.

Murky brown water, sucking mud, and tall reeds filled with clouds of whining mosquitoes stretch away into the vast distances of the Great Swamp.

"We'll never find our way through this mess!" you exclaim angrily.

"Of course we will. I used to come here every day gathering lotus bulbs," says Saffron as she strides confidently into the swamp. "Don't worry. I know the way."

You hack at tall weeds with your staff. Somehow it doesn't seem right that you, a graduate magic-user and almost an adult, should be led by a little girl and her man-eating cat. It's—it's downright embarrassing!

"Morgan," Hinoki links gently, "the wise person accepts help when he needs it, from wherever it is offered."

"And I'm not a little girl!" Saffron declares indignantly. "If you think you're so wonderful, Mr. Almost Grown-up Magic-user, you can guide us yourself!"

"Can't I think anything without the two of you jumping all over me? The next thing I know, Grundoon will be telling me what to do! And what's so hard about guiding? I'll bet I'd do just fine!" And pushing your way to the front, you set off in a new direction.

"Morgan!" chides Hinoki, but you do not answer. Saffron follows reluctantly.

All day long you trudge from one mound of mud to the next until you are forced to admit that you are hopelessly lost.

"What do I do now?" you groan inwardly as you sink wearily down on a tuft of grass.

"You could come and rescue me," whispers an unknown voice inside your head.

"Oh, no! Not another one!" you moan, holding your aching head.

"It's coming from over there, off to the right," says Hinoki as he spreads his wings and flaps upward. "Morgan, come quickly!" he urges.

Pulling yourself up, you slog through the scummy water toward Hinoki's voice, with Saffron splashing alongside you. As you part a curtain of marsh grass, you see an amazing sight. There, sprawled in the mud, is a great feathered serpent—a couatl! Although you have heard of them, you have never seen one before. You know they are extremely powerful, both in magic and in strength. It is hard to imagine one being hurt, yet here one lies before you, sprawled helplessly in the mud.

Slipping to the couatl's side, Saffron places a slender arm under its body and cradles its head in her lap. Stroking the dull scales, she asks, "Can you tell us what happened?"

"It was done by a magic-user—one whose soul and mind are black and bent," groans the couatl. "I was patrolling the swamp—it is part of the territory I protect—when I felt his thoughts. I challenged him and asked him his purpose and his destination, as is my right. Instead of answering, he attacked me mentally.

"I was stunned," the couatl goes on, "but I protected myself and then we fought. I have

never met anyone whose strength equalled
mine. Indeed, he was stronger. At last, he
laughed and left me for dead, knowing I was too
weak to call for help or fly away. Never in my
lifetime have I encountered such strength or felt
such evil! You must help me. I must prevent this
evil magic-user from carrying out his plans. He
means to destroy the world!''

1) If you want to help the couatl, turn to page
   114.

2) If you're not sure you can help the couatl
   and think you should push on after Zed,
   turn to page 67.

You reach out to try to lift the lid, and suddenly the chest vanishes before your eyes, and you find yourself falling into a pit.

"It was an illusion trap!" shouts Hinoki as you both fall into the pit and begin to slide on some kind of smooth surface.

Before you can even catch your breath, the slide ends and you land heavily on a floor of shiny black marble.

"Look at this place!" you murmur as you stare about you in awe.

High, high above you, the ceiling fades into darkness. Great black marble pillars, carved into arches, line both sides of the immense room, so large you can't even see its edges. Gold-bracketed torches on each pillar light the room. Reflected in their glow, the room gleams, almost blinding you with its black brilliance.

"Hinoki, look! It's like a million mirrors. Every time I move, all the images of me move, too. What is it made of? Where are we?"

"It's faceted, highly polished black onyx," links Hinoki. "As to where we are, I don't know, although the fact that it is all black has me worried."

"It's not all black," you say, pointing to the floor, which is heaped with precious gems, fine jewelry, gold coins, armor—and skeletons.

"Look Morgan, there's even a magic item. It's a bag of holding!" Hinoki links excitedly.

Following the little dragon's gaze, you cross the shifting masses of treasure and stand beside the skeleton of the unfortunate fighter who apparently once owned the magic item. Forcing yourself to remember that he is long dead and cannot harm you, you bend down and pick up the deceptively small bag of holding.

"This is a great and wonderful item, Morgan," links Hinoki. "You might have had to wait for years before obtaining one on your own."

"True," you say, "but it didn't seem to do this fellow much good. And we still have to get out of here."

As you put the bag of holding in your pocket, you hear strange, thin whistling, and the hair on the back of your neck rises instantly.

"Morgan, the torches are flickering!" links Hinoki.

"Does it feel cold in here?" you ask as you listen to the strange whistling noise rise and fall. Covering your ears, you try to block out the eerie wailing.

"Morgan, look!" whispers Hinoki. And raising your eyes, you tremble with fear as you behold a terrifying sight. Striding toward you out of the black arches is a snakelike mass, approximately fifteen feet tall, that seems to be composed of icy clouds. Its cheeks are swollen full, and from its lips issues a terrible cold wind that blows straight toward you. As the wind sweeps through the hall, it covers everything it touches with ice and snow.

"It's a wind walker," you whisper in dread. "What should we do?"

"Think, Morgan! What kind of spells do you have left that could help us?"

"I can't think of anything. Everything that might work is at least fifth level, and I'm not that good yet."

"Can't you use the bag of holding?" links Hinoki as he hides behind your head and peers out nervously.

"I guess I can," you say slowly. "The bag is pretty simple. I'll have to try."

Suddenly the wind walker stops, fills its cheeks full, and blows directly at you.

Running as fast as you can on the shifting mounds of treasure, you race for one of the pillars and dive behind it just as the blast of icy air strikes.

As you rub your arms frantically, trying to regain some warmth, Hinoki links, "Quick, Morgan, do something! We'll never survive another blast like that!"

Peering from behind the arch, you watch the wind walker fill its cheeks once more.

There is only one thing to do. You have to try using the bag of holding to trap the thing.

Please turn to page 125.

You lunge forward, jabbing at the monster with your staff. The staff scrapes along the creature's snout harmlessly. Its fanged jaws open wide and loom over your head. Desperately you try to fend off the terrifying creature. Instantly the snaky head whips down, wrenches the staff from your hands, and crunches it into kindling.

"Help!" screams Saffron. Risking a quick glance, you see one of the creature's heads rising up into the mist, gripping the edge of Saffron's long skirt in its teeth.

"Morgan, do something!" cries Hinoki as he bravely flies into one of the monster's faces in an attempt to distract it.

Seizing the chance, you break off a dry branch from a nearby tree and fling yourself under the monster. Desperately you jab the sharp end of the branch directly up into the soft underportion of its body. Your hope is shortlived as the branch strikes hard bone and breaks. Then, roaring with rage, the hydra bends down, plucks you out of the water, and shakes you furiously.

As Hinoki flutters helplessly, the hydra turns and stalks off into the gloom, with you and Saffron firmly in its jaws.

The world spins around you. You realize that you have made the wrong decision. Maybe there is still a way to free yourself, but in all likelihood, this is . . .

THE END

You approach the pedestal and touch the sapphire lightly with one finger. It feels warm. Hot, even.

Hinoki breaks his silence and says, "I don't think you should push that button," and then flies up and sits on the statue's wing.

You've had the same thoughts, but having Hinoki tell you what to do makes you angry.

"I'll do as I please," you say, and looking away from him, you push the button.

A thick column of flame shoots out from the dragon's mouth, and you disappear as though you never existed.

For a long time, Hinoki sits on the statue, grieving for you. "I was only angry with him. I just wanted him to learn a little lesson, not to get killed," he says sadly.

THE END

"I'm tired," you say as you rub your aching leg muscles. "We haven't stopped to sleep or eat for more than two days now, ever since we started following this trail to the north."

"I'm not tired," says Hinoki.

"Of course not. You've been riding on my shoulder ever since we left home. But I need to stop to eat and get a good night's sleep, or I won't be able to go any farther. Then we can continue on after Uncle Zed."

"I could use something to eat, too," says Hinoki. "Why don't I fly ahead and see what I can find?"

"All right," you say as you sink to the floor of the forest. "Come back and tell me something good."

You rest your head against a large, shaggy tree and watch as the small dragon flaps skyward. Soon images of distant treetops and rolling countryside start to flash through your mind. You see a whitewashed building, thatched with fresh rushes, and a sign blowing in the wind.

"That building looks like it might be an inn. Get a little closer to it so I can see what it is," you direct.

"I agree with—" Hinoki's voice begins inside your head, and then his words break off, and you see the horizon flash by at incredible speed. The forest draws closer and closer, and then branches and leaves flash by in your mind almost faster than you can see them. You close your eyes and throw your arms up in front of

your face, even though you know that you are
only seeing what Hinoki sees and cannot be
harmed. Suddenly there is a great snap, and the
picture fades.

"How many times do I have to tell you not to
do that to me?" you shout as Hinoki drops onto
your shoulder. "If you're going to do that, break
the mind link! You know I get airsick!"

"I'm sorry, Morgan. I forgot. And what would
you have me do—order a meal at the inn and eat
it on a plate with silverware?"

Quarreling amicably, the two of you continue
on toward the building you saw through Hinoki's eyes.

"Maybe our luck's going to change," you say
as you look at the sign that shows a roasted duck
and a mug of ale. "TRAVELERS WELCOME"
reads the sign.

The last rays of the setting sun light your
way to the front door of the inn. The latch gives
way beneath your hand, and you see a large
whitewashed room. Heavy beams cross the low
ceiling, and hanging from each beam are mugs
of copper, pewter, and bronze. A hearty fire
crackles on the hearth, and the aroma of roast
lamb fills the air.

"May I help you, sir?" asks a small, nervous
voice.

"Oh, there you are," you say, eyeing the hag-
gard man who suddenly appears at your side.
"I'd like a good dinner, a bed for the night—and
some information."

"Dinner? Bed? Information?" repeats the

innkeeper, wringing his hands nervously.

"What's the matter with this fellow? He's acting very strange," Hinoki's voice says inside your head.

"Yes," you repeat. "A bed for the night, dinner, and some information. I am looking for my uncle. He's very, very old, and his name is Zed. Perhaps he stopped here. It's the only northbound road leading out of the mountains, and we know he came this way."

Before the words are even out of your mouth, the innkeeper is shaking his head from side to side. "No beds," he says. "We're full up. And we've nothing to eat. Not a crumb in the place. And I've never seen your uncle. He's never been here. I'm positive. You'll have to leave now. I was just closing."

"What are you talking about?" you cry angrily. "There's not a soul in the place besides us, and I smell roast lamb. And why would you be closing? It's barely nightfall. As for leaving, why, it's starting to rain. I'm cold, tired, and hungry, and I have no desire to sleep in some wet woods when I can stay here."

The innkeeper wrings his hands and twitches nervously. Suddenly a smaller figure, no higher than his shoulder, appears in the doorway behind him. Although the figure's narrow face is covered with smudges of soot and hundreds of freckles, you decide that the creature is a girl. Her head is covered with a tight mat of red-gold curls that look as though they have been hacked at with a dull knife. Her clothes are a mismatched mess of patches and wrinkles. Only the brightest blues eyes you have ever seen save the girl from looking like a walking ragbag.

"We will stay here tonight," you say firmly. Unseen by the innkeeper, the girl shakes her head from side to side.

"I'm sorry, sir. You should leave," insists the innkeeper. The girl nods in agreement, her eyes never leaving your face.

"The child seems to be trying to tell us something," says Hinoki's voice. "Why don't we do what she says? Sleeping in the woods won't kill us. There's something odd going on around here."

1) If you want to follow Hinoki's and the strange girl's advice, turn to page 68.

2) If you insist on staying at the inn, turn to page 123.

You enter a large room and collapse on a wide shelf. You hear a muffled sound, and two openings, about the size of your head, open in the wall beside you. There is a rattling noise, and greenish brown objects the size of melons cascade into the container behind you. The container is no sooner filled than a torrent of silvery blue fluid pours from the second opening and fills the other container to the brim.

Your exhaustion wins out over your curiosity, and for a period of time you sleep as Hinoki stands guard.

When at last you awaken, you are stiff but well rested. "Where are we? What is this place?" you ask between dry, cracked lips.

"I suspect it is some sort of food supply room for dragons," links Hinoki. "I think you should try some dragon pellets and water. You'll feel better."

"Dragon pellets?" you whisper as you stagger over to the containers.

Although you are not tall enough to see into them, your shoulders are too sore to fly, so you climb laboriously up the side of the first bowl. Spurred on by the thought of food and drink, you succeed in reaching the top, where you teeter on the rim. You bend over, trying to reach the crystalline liquid, but no matter how you position yourself, you can't reach it.

Clinging tightly to the rim with both hands, you lower yourself farther and farther, until you lose your balance and fall into the bowl with a splash.

You open your mouth to yell, and sweet, cool liquid gushes in. It tastes vaguely of cinnamon and spearmint and is slightly thicker than water. You swallow and instantly, a contented warmth radiates through you. At last, marvelously refreshed, you climb out of the bowl. You fly over to the next container, sit down on the rim, and pick up one of the pellets.

"This is great! What do you suppose this stuff is?"

"Hmmm . . . probably a mixture of bone meal, dried blood, grass, and charcoal to clean the teeth and purify the breath," links Hinoki. "You know, just regular dragon pellets—nothing fancy."

Gagging, you put down the remainder of your dragon pellet and feel yourself turning slightly green. "Why didn't you tell me?" you gasp.

"Why? What's the matter? I liked it," links Hinoki, grinning.

Before you can answer, there is a great rush of wind and a large gray dragon flies into the room and lands on the platform with a thump.

"Oh! Who are you?" squeaks the dragon in a high, thin voice. It is easy to see that the newcomer is terrified of you. Tiny as you are, next to her, she cowers in obvious fear.

"Peace, sister. We won't hurt you," says Hinoki, and the drab gray dragon turns her sorrowful gaze toward him. You can see the doubt in her eyes.

"Honestly, we wouldn't hurt you," you say sincerely. "Why, you could squash me flat in an

instant if you wanted to. You're far more dangerous to me than I am to you. We're here on a mission, not to bring harm to dragons. Please don't
be afraid."

Edging around you, the dragon drinks deeply
from the bowl of water, never taking her eyes
from you for a second. As she drinks, her scales
gradually change from dingy gray to sparkling
silver, shot with shimmering irridescence. Her
crest and wings, moments earlier hanging in
ragged tatters about her body, seem to reweave
themselves.

The dragon laps two full bowls of the healing
fluid before she moves on to the bowl of dragon
pellets. She does not take her eyes from you
until she has consumed her fill.

Only when she begins to groom herself with
her long pink tongue does Hinoki speak. "Will
you tell us what frightens you so?"

The dragon stares at the two of you long
before she answers. "I am not anxious to share
anything with humans, unless it is my flame.
Nor am I pleased to find a human here. But
because you ask, I will tell you, even though I
think your choice of friends poor.

"My name is Pearl. My home is in the Smoke
Mountains, far from here. I returned, as I do
yearly, to visit old friends, retell old tales, and
weave new ones. But since I arrived, there has
been only the scent of danger and fear.

"Many of my old friends have not returned,
and those who have tell tales of treachery and
death. The Dragon of Doom is loose in the land,

and all that was once safe is safe no more. It is said that a certain human is to blame.

"No good will come of it. The Dragon of Doom neither fears nor obeys anyone. Now that he is unleashed, we shall all suffer."

"What happened to you, Pearl? How did you come to be injured?" asks Hinoki.

"When I heard the tales, I decided to come directly to the Grand Dragon and ask him if there is any truth to the matter. But when I arrived at the castle, all was different.

"I was challenged at the entrance, and my right wing was badly burned by the guardian. Why in dragondom would the guardian burn a dragon?

"And then, after I passed the door, I fell into a trap. A trap!" squeaks Pearl angrily. "Who would set a trap for a dragon inside Dragon Castle!

"My wing could barely hold me after I hurt it in the fall. I knew that this station was here, and I forced myself to fly on. I almost didn't make it."

Your heart aches with sympathy as you listen to Pearl's sad story. "Pearl, the stories you have heard are true. The Dragon of Doom has been called forth by my uncle, who I fear has gone mad. I will do everything in my power to stop him from carrying out his evil plan, which is to end the world as we all know it."

Pearl draws back in horror at your words. Finally, in a choked voice she says, "You must get to the Great Dragon. I fear that no matter how great your resolve, you will not be able to stop them. Perhaps the Great Dragon will help you."

"Who is the Great Dragon?" you ask.

Pearl turns disapproving eyes on Hinoki. "You have not educated this human well!" she says. Then, turning her gaze back to you, she explains carefully, as though speaking to a small child. "The Great Dragon rules over all dragons on this and any other plane of existence. All matters of importance to dragonkind are resolved by him. He is all-knowing and all-powerful and very, very wise."

"Well, he sounds like our man—uh, our dragon, that is. How do I get to him?"

"I was going there," answers Pearl. "If you would like to accompany me, I'll show you the way."

Please turn to page 102.

"I cannot let you do this to Hinoki," you say bravely. "He only came along to help me. Hinoki, go back to the council and tell them exactly what has happened. Maybe it's not too late to send someone else. And, Hinoki? Please remember me."

"Morgan, don't do this!" Hinoki links unevenly. "There's got to be another way! You can't leave me. I'll stay with you."

"No, Hinoki. You go back to the council. I must stay here. It's the only way."

Hinoki winds himself tightly around your neck, and for an instant, your resolve weakens. Your tears mingle with his, and then you place him at the dragon's feet and say, "I am ready."

The dragon stares at you coldly. "Is this some kind of a trick?" it asks at last.

"There is no trick!" you say firmly.

"You would really do this for a dragon?" breathes the Great Dragon, surprised.

"I just said I would," you say.

"It doesn't seem right. No one's ever won before," says the dragon.

"You mean you're not going to put me in that globe?" you ask in amazement.

"I can still do it if you want me to," murmurs the dragon.

"No!" you exclaim. "Does this mean I've won and you're going to help us?"

"I know of this evil man, Zed," says the dragon. "He must be stopped. He is destroying the balance between good and evil. The balance between the two is always delicate, and here at

Dragon Castle, we can only exist if we maintain the balance. Were evil to gain the upper hand, Dragon Castle would disappear forever, taking with it the only safe haven for dragons. Dragons would never be safe again. What do you know about this Zed?"

Quickly you tell your story, with Hinoki prompting you.

"The Dragon of Doom here! We must act before it is too late!"

"It is already too late to stop me!" cracks a voice more ancient than time itself. And out of the shadows of the room steps the wrinkled form of Zed. Despite his size, he seems to have an aura around him.

"It is too late!" he repeats with a smile. "Shen is here this very minute!"

A great wind sweeps through the room, and you grow cold with fear. You clutch Hinoki to you tightly.

The dragon that settles before you is twice as large as the great silver dragon and much, much more frightening. Not even its missing scales, its ancient scars, its shattered claws, and its tattered crest lessens the impression of power and majesty.

"Why have you come?" asks the silver dragon.

"End the world now!" screams Zed. "Wipe it clean of my enemies!" And at his words, the room seems to quake under your feet.

"No! You must not!" you cry, rushing forward.

"You must do my bidding! It was I who called you forth!" raves Zed. "You must do as I say!"

"I obey no man!" the dragon intones ominously. "You may ask, but you may not command. I will hear what the child has to say. Perhaps I will like his words better than yours! Speak, child of man!"

"P-Please, sir, don't do what he says!"

"And what would you ask of me, manchild? Who would you have me kill?"

"No one, sir. I don't want to kill anyone."

"Surely there is someone you would have me kill. What about your uncle? His plans for death would have included you. Do you not wish him dead?" rasps the dragon.

"Oh, no!" you say. "I'm supposed to bring him back to the council. He's a great man, really he is! He's—he's just angry!"

"Not all of mankind is as evil as this wicked man," says Hinoki. "It is true that you seldom see any but those who are evil and greedy and think only of themselves, but much of mankind is good, Great Shen. It would be sad if man were to disappear because one evil man wishes it so."

"Wisely spoken," says the Dragon of Doom slowly. "What would you have me do?"

"Do! You must do as I command!" screams Zed.

"SILENCE!" roars Shen, enveloping Zed in a cloud of steam. Then, turning to Hinoki, Shen repeats. "What would you have me do?"

"I am only a small dragon," says Hinoki. "But I do not wish to end the world."

"Nor do I," sighs Shen. "I am weary of man and his petty plots. I leave the world and its fate in your hands. I have carried the burden long enough. Go back to your people, manchild, and tell them that the Dragon of Doom is gone—forever, perhaps. What becomes of man is no longer my concern."

"But what of me!" rages Zed.

"For you, I have special plans," breathes Shen. And rising slowly, he clutches Zed in the coils of his tail. "You shall return with me to my cave at the End of the World. There is treasure there—more treasure than you can imagine! But you will have no use for treasure—not ever again."

Then slowly, with great majesty, the mighty Shen, the Dragon of Doom, rises slowly and disappears from the world, never to be seen again.

THE END

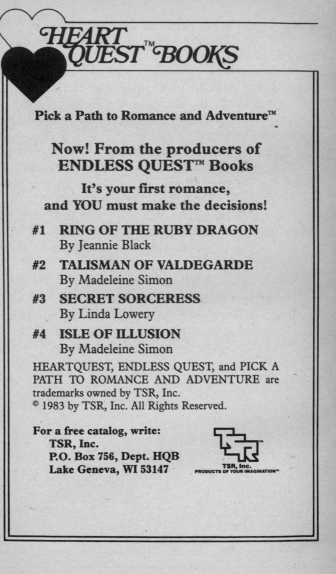